He narrowed his eyes, as though he didn't trust her. She suspected pirates trusted no one.

"Why offer me something of value for something with none?" the pirate asked, his voice laced with suspicion.

"The pendant was my mother's. She died recently, and it's all I have left to remember her by."

"The pirate way is to take the finger when we take the ring. If you want to keep your lovely hand whole, you'll have to give me something else of value."

Annalisa swallowed hard at the thought of losing her finger, but she couldn't deny the truth. "I have nothing else."

He grinned. A grin more terrifying than his eyes or his dagger. "Oh, but I think you do."

# To Catch A Pirate

## JADE PARKER

Point

ISBN-13: 978-0-439-02694-9
ISBN-10: 0-439-02694-6

12  11  10  9  8  7  6  5  4  3  2  1
            7  8  9  10  11  12/0

Printed in the U.S.A.                    01
First printing, May 2007

To Catch
A Pirate

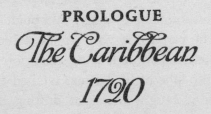

*The Caribbean 1720*

Annalisa Townsend didn't know which terrified her more: the razor-sharp edge of the dagger pressed against her throat or the ruthless glare of the pirate who'd shoved her against the wall with the harsh words, "Hold your tongue or I'll remove it."

The glare, she decided. It belonged to a young man she sensed was not familiar with mercy, given or received. He was breathing heavily, having run down the stairs into the ship's hold only seconds earlier.

A thin diagonal scar marred his right cheek. While it failed to detract from what might have been a devilishly handsome face in a London ballroom, here in the open waters of the

Caribbean it served to create the most frightening visage she'd ever encountered.

The young man had covered his head with a dark red scarf; his midnight black hair — unfashionably long, although she doubted he cared one whit about fashion — curled along his shoulders. A small gold ring through the lobe of his left ear winked at her whenever it caught the light drifting down from the opening at the top of the stairs. The simple jewelry somehow made him appear all the more menacing.

She didn't think he was much older than her sixteen years, but his dark green eyes were far more ancient and revealed a life that had known little except hardship. In spite of the sweltering heat, chills erupted along her skin and caused her to shiver. She knew compassion was not in his nature. He was as ruthless as the barbaric pirates who'd attacked the ship.

He was, after all, one of them.

Annalisa had been traveling on the *Horizon* with her father. King George had assigned him the governorship of Mourning, a small, little-known island in the Caribbean. She'd thought the assignment appropriate since she and her father were still reeling from the recent unexpected death of her mother, who had succumbed to the fever. Annalisa was grateful to have an excuse to leave behind England and the sorrowful memories of losing her mother.

She'd been looking forward to this adventure. She'd never before traveled on the sea, and found it thrilling. She began to fall in love with the balmy sea air as they drew closer to her new home. She cherished the fact that it didn't smell of illness or death. When she breathed it in deeply, she found a measure of peace.

But that was before the pirates had attacked.

She couldn't help but think their ship, *Phantom Mist*, was appropriately named; it had seemed to appear out of nowhere.

Unlike the familiar black flag flown by most pirate ships, a red one waved atop this one. Annalisa had overheard the crew talking in low voices with obvious dread. A red flag signaled no mercy would be asked for, and none would be given.

From all accounts, the pirates' captain, Crimson Kelly, was as ruthless a man as ever sailed the high seas. It was debated whether his name came from his flaming red hair and beard or from his ghastly penchant for filling

3

his wine goblet with blood drained from his victims.

When *Horizon*'s captain had announced they were too weighted down with cargo to escape the rapidly approaching ship, Annalisa's father ordered her to hide in the cargo hold. She'd wanted to defy him, but she'd known she would be no help during the battle. She knew only that the pointy end of the cutlass was the dangerous end.

So she'd scurried into the hold, located a nearly empty crate, and crawled inside, pulling the top over her. But hidden in the darkness, hearing the booming of cannons, the crack of splintering wood, and the ringing of clashing steel rage above her, not knowing about her father's fate became too much to bear. Leaving the safety of the crate, she'd been creeping toward the stairs when the young pirate came barreling down them.

She'd barely had time to turn before he grabbed her and pinned her against the wall.

Now, the distant sound of battle settled into an ominous hush. A heartbeat later, yells of triumph echoed. Annalisa knew the fighting was over. Her heart sank with the knowledge. The pirates had won. All that remained was the pillaging, the looting, the destroying. She heard the thuds, the crashes as the plundering began. All would be torn asunder.

And what of her father? Had they killed him? She had to know. If he was alive she wanted to feel his arms around her. And if he was dead or dying she wanted to wrap her arms around him, to offer what little comfort she could.

"Please —" she began.

"Silence. I'll not say it again. Hold your tongue or lose it."

She was surprised by his accent. British, to be sure, but more refined than she'd expected. The voice of one destined to be a gentleman. What role had fate played in turning him into a pirate? She felt ashamed to be intrigued by the circumstances that had shaped him. He was a blackguard. All she should want was to be free of him.

Slowly, his gaze roamed over her face, almost as though he was trying to memorize it. Did they take women captives? Would they sell her into slavery? She'd heard of such things, but she didn't know if anything could be worse than being wedged between the wall and him.

His gaze dipped to the gold pendant that

hung just below her throat. With his free hand, he slipped his fingers around it. . . .

"No, please, I beg of you, have mercy, don't take it," she said quickly, desperately, overcoming her fear of his threats to cut out her tongue. "It's only a cheap trinket."

His gaze shot up, his eyes boring into hers. "You dare defy me?"

Swallowing hard, fighting back tears, she shook her head. "I only sought to explain."

"You don't value your tongue?"

"I value the necklace more."

Her answer seemed to surprise him.

"Sterling!" a far-off voice shouted.

The pirate's attention darted toward the opening at the top of the stairs. Light drifted from above into the hold. She could see the concentration in his face. She thought she might even have a chance of escaping. But before she could take action, he shifted his gaze back to her, and he seemed more menacing than before. "I have to take something up or Crimson Kelly will be down here himself. He'll take far more than your precious piece."

"Here," she said, breathlessly, holding up her right hand, showing him the ring she wore on her third finger. "Take it. It's got diamonds, much more valuable."

He narrowed his eyes as though he didn't trust her. She suspected pirates trusted no one.

"Why offer me something of greater value?" he asked, his voice laced with suspicion.

"The pendant was my mother's. She died recently, and it's all I have left to remember her by."

"You want to remember her?"

It seemed an odd question.

"Of course. Why would I not?"

He looked on the verge of providing an answer before shaking his head and appearing to think better of it.

"The pirate way is to take the finger when we take the ring. If you want to keep your lovely hand whole, you'll have to give me something else of value."

She swallowed hard at the thought of losing her finger, but she couldn't deny the truth. "I have nothing else."

He grinned. A grin more terrifying than his eyes or his dagger. "Oh, but I think you do."

Before she could protest, he lowered his head and kissed her. Hard. On the mouth.

She'd never before been kissed like this. To her immense surprise, his lips were warm and eager. He tasted of . . . apples. Tart and sweet. She wondered if he'd been munching on one before the attack.

Then the kiss grew more passionate, more demanding. Her toes curled. Her knees weakened, and she found herself clutching him, in fear of falling.

For a moment, she almost forgot he was a pirate.

"James Sterling! Where ye be, matey? If ye were careless enough to get yerself killed, I'll be drinkin' your blood with me supper tonight!"

The pirate drew back, grabbed her hand, and yanked her ring from her finger. Chuckling as though he was privy to some immense joke, he stepped away from her, backing toward the stairs.

"A fair trade, m'lady. I'm content with it."

Pressing her trembling hand to her moistened lips, she stared at him. His laughter abruptly ended, his expression turned solemn and harsh.

"Now, hide until we've left," he commanded.

He turned on his heel and dashed up the stairs. "I'm here, Crimson! Nothing of value in the hold!"

Somehow Annalisa made it back into the crate without her quivering legs giving out. Once inside and with the top pulled into place, she curled into a quivering ball. Tears burned her eyes. Had she just sealed her coffin?

She flinched every time she heard a crash or a bang. And she prayed, prayed desperately, for salvation.

She didn't know how long she waited, but eventually she became aware of the silence. And it terrified her. What could it mean? Had the pirates left?

She'd lifted the lid only a bit when she heard footsteps thundering down the stairs.

"Miss Townsend! Miss Townsend!"

She recognized the voice. Nathaniel Northrup. One of the younger officers. He was undeniably handsome, with curling blond hair and brown eyes. Although he seldom spoke to her, several times she'd caught him watching her from afar when she was strolling about the deck.

"Here! I'm here!" she shouted.

She was pushing back the top when suddenly it was thrown off and Mr. Northrup was staring down at her, his expression serious. His clothing and face were streaked with blood.

"Your father sent me to fetch you," he told her as he helped her clamber out.

Immense relief swept through her. "Oh, thank goodness. Is he all right?"

"He's hurt but alive. We're abandoning ship."

"Why?"

"Because the pirates set it afire. Come, we must hurry!"

He grabbed her hand. His legs were longer than hers, and she had a difficult time keeping up with his frantic pace as he tugged her up the stairs. When they reached the top, she thought she might be sick. Mangled bodies littered the deck.

"Don't look," Nathaniel ordered.

How could she not? If she didn't, she'd trip over them.

He urged her across the deck, to where Captain Hawthorne was standing. "I'm glad to see you're safe, Miss Townsend," he said. "Your father's waiting."

Looking over the side of the ship, she saw the longboat. It was one of four that had already been lowered into the water. Her father and several crewmen were sitting in it as it bobbed on the sea.

"How do I get down there?" she asked.

"You just climb down Jacob's ladder," Captain Hawthorne said, lifting a rope ladder and letting it drop back against the side. "Mr. Northrup will go first, then you, soon enough after him so he's there to prevent you from falling. I'll follow once you're safely in the boat. Over the side now, lad. Hurry. The longboat must get away before the ship sinks or it's in danger of being pulled under."

Annalisa watched as Nathaniel Northrup climbed over the side of the ship, holding firm to the ladder, waiting for her to join him. The captain helped her climb over the side to join Nathaniel.

It was awkward with him so near, but his presence also gave her the confidence to step down quickly. When they were close enough to the longboat, hanging on with one hand, he swung himself to the side, guiding her as other hands took hold of her and helped her into the boat. When she finally settled in beside her father, she wound her arms around him.

"You're safe," she whispered brokenly. "Thank goodness, you're safe."

"They took the ivory chest, Anna. The one King George entrusted to me. His Majesty won't think well of me for letting it be taken."

She knew gold coins that were to be used to build a splendid palace and fort on Mourning had been stored inside. Mourning was a newly acquired island, and King George had plans for it to be the jewel of the Caribbean. The king had suggested that British men-of-war accompany the *Horizon*. But her father had argued against it. He thought an escort would alert pirates that he was carrying something precious. He didn't want them sacking Mourning before he'd even begun to build its first township.

Annalisa pulled back. "What choice did you have? Surely he'll understand, Father."

But her father didn't seem to be listening. He stared straight ahead as though witnessing something horrible.

The boat rocked as Captain Hawthorne boarded it. "Let's be off, men!" he shouted. "Row handsomely now!"

The crewmen began rowing. It was only then that Annalisa noticed Nathaniel sitting across from her. It took all her strength to give him a shaky smile.

"You're trembling," he said.

"I'm freezing. Isn't that s-s-silly?" she stammered. "We're in the Caribbean and I feel as though I've been buried in snow."

He removed his jacket and placed it around her shoulders. "Your reaction is quite normal," he said. "You've had a terrifying experience. I'm a bit shaky myself."

The smile she gave him this time was a little more solid. She absorbed the warmth of his jacket, hardly noticing the blood that still marred it.

As the men rowed them farther out, she glanced back toward the *Horizon*, watching in horror as flames engulfed the ship and all the lost souls who remained aboard.

Then she looked toward the south where another ship sailed boldly away. She thought of the pirate who'd accosted her in the hold.

James Sterling. She'd remember his name. She'd remember his face.

And worst of all, she'd never forget his kiss.

## CHAPTER ONE

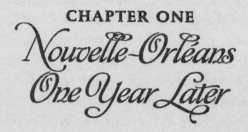

# Nouvelle-Orléans
# One Year Later

James Sterling was a pirate without a ship.

Sitting in a shadowy corner at the back of the crowded tavern, he reached for his tankard of grog, cursing the fact that he was in this wretched part of the world.

Aboard the *Phantom Mist*, he'd thought he found a place where he belonged. He enjoyed the feel of a ship beneath him. He welcomed the challenge of storms, man against nature. He even relished the dangers to be found in pirating: the risks of battle, the threat of being captured, the chance of being hanged, the opportunity to acquire wealth beyond his wildest dreams.

Yet here he was, condemned to a life on

land, a man with a bounty on his head and no ship at his beck and call.

He downed the remainder of his grog and slammed the tankard onto the table. Peering through the smoke-filled haze, he caught the attention of the harried barmaid standing nearby and held up two fingers. She gave him a wink, a bright smile, and a quick nod. He knew two more brews would be forthcoming.

Leaning back in his chair, he toyed with the ring he wore on the little finger of his left hand. A more worthless trinket he'd never known. Fool's gold and cut glass. It had cost him everything: the life he loved, the danger he craved, the respect of his captain.

Worse still, the girl he'd discovered in the hold continued to haunt him.

He didn't even know her name, but she'd earned his admiration. Even with his dagger pressed to her throat, she'd been defiant, fire blazing in her eyes, a blue so bright that not even the shadows could dim them. Her brown hair spilling over her shoulders no doubt enticed many a man. He was no exception.

Devil take it, but he dreamed of holding her in his arms. Since that fateful day, no other female had caught his fancy. The girl was a witch, capable of casting a spell over him. It was the only explanation. Why else could he not forget her?

The buxom barmaid set two tankards on his table. With a wink, he flipped a coin her way.

She gave him a smile of invitation. "After we close, I can offer more zan tankards to a handsome lad like yourself."

James grinned. "Thanks for the offer, but I most likely will be otherwise occupied later."

She angled her head thoughtfully. "You look familiar, *mon ami*."

"Can't imagine why I would. I'm a stranger to these parts."

"Still, zere's something about you." She shook her head as though to clear it. "It'll come to me. If you change your mind about later . . ." Leaving the remainder of the invitation unspoken, she turned and walked away. James had no plans to change his mind.

"Is one of 'em fer me, matey?"

James had been so absorbed observing the wench, he'd missed the arrival of Ferret, so named because he had a talent for ferreting out information.

Wrapping his hand around a tankard, James scooted it across the scarred wooden table. It looked as though many a man had carelessly taken a knife to it. "'Course, mate."

Licking his lips, Ferret dropped into the chair nearest James, bringing the odor of rotting fish and stale sweat with him. Ferret ̣ d been a worthy pirate before they'd attacked the *Horizon*. But one of the crewmen, fighting valiantly, had slashed Ferret's arm. With a festering wound, he'd been declared useless and, along with James, marooned on a deserted island in the Caribbean. James had been forced to watch Ferret die or finish off what the enemy started. He'd finished the task . . . and no doubt ended Ferret's career as a useful pirate.

"More's the pity it wasn't me right arm," Ferret had said, once he recovered. "The pay's better fer a right arm."

It was like Ferret to grumble over the loss of coin more than the loss of limb. While James couldn't deny that pirates were dastardly fellows, they did look after their own. A man was compensated for loss of limb, unless he had the misfortune of serving under a captain who would abandon him at the first sight of inconvenience. Which Ferret had.

As had James. While the *Horizon* was burning, Crimson had held a spyglass to his eye, taking pleasure in the destruction he'd wrought. While he attacked ships of all nations, he was in the habit of always burning British ships. Where they were concerned, he held a particular dislike.

As was his habit, James had been standing beside him, careful not to show the relief he felt when he saw the longboat moving beyond the hulking ship and brown hair blowing in the wind.

Crimson considered himself James's teacher and liked to keep him close. James had started out as his cabin boy, keeping everything tidy and clean. He learned a lot from Crimson. Most were lessons hard learned, but learned nonetheless.

"There looks to be a wench aboard," Crimson growled. "How'd we miss 'er?"

"She musta been hiding," James said.

"We tore the ship apart, from stem to stern. Someone had to have seen 'er. I'm bettin' she was in the 'old."

Crimson gave him a hard glare, the kind of look that caused lesser blokes to cry for their mothers. It never signaled anything good.

James dug the ring out of his pocket. "She paid me well to let her go."

Crimson snatched up the ring, studied it, and tossed it back to James. "It's naught but glass, lad. A bit of fakery. We'll see how well you think she paid you when I'm done with you."

James realized then that he should have taken the necklace. Hell, he should have taken the girl. She was a prize worthy of any pirate.

Now all James possessed was the reminder of his foolishness.

It was months before a merchant ship had neared the island where they'd been abandoned and seen their signal fires. Six months of eating fish and lizards. When they made their first port, they'd jumped ship. Since that time, it had been a game of cat and mouse, hiding aboard one ship after another, trying to evade the pirate hunter who was spreading reward notices for James all along the coast. Six weeks ago, James and Ferret had arrived in French Louisiana. The ship that brought them was in port for repairs. It would be a few more weeks before it was ready to head back into open waters. James wasn't of a mind to wait. Nor did he particularly care for life aboard an honest ship. It involved a good deal of work for very little pay.

Before Ferret could grab his tankard, James snatched it back. "Did you do as I asked?"

"I did. I swear." He leaned toward James. "It's as ye suspected. The pirate hunter is on our scent. *The Dangerous Lady* made port late this afternoon."

James was already well aware of that.

"They say the cap'n be a woman who be equally dangerous," Ferret began.

"So I've heard."

"But yer not believin' it. I can tell, but I've known women pirates." He winked. "Known 'em very well, if you catch my drift."

"But not privateers. No royal governor would issue a letter of marque to a woman. He'd be laughed out of office."

"But what if he did?"

"Then he's an idiot."

"That goes without saying, if ye ask me."

"I'm not asking you."

"Ye think she's lying about the marque?" Ferret asked.

James shrugged, thinking of his mother. "All women lie. All women betray."

"Aye," Ferret said, grinning. "But ye got to forgive 'em. Where else ye gonna get a kiss?"

James shook his head, wishing Ferret hadn't mentioned kisses. It had been too long since James had kissed a girl, and that last kiss haunted him still. *"The Dangerous Lady* is not captained by a woman."

"Believe what you will." Ferret reached into his jacket, removed a piece of paper, and awkwardly unfolded it with his one hand. "Woman or no, she's passing these around. She's after you, ye know."

He did know. It was the reason they were living in the shadows of the recently built port city.

James took the paper and studied his likeness, etched on the reward notice beneath the amount of one hundred pounds. It was like staring into a looking glass, so accurate was the portrait. Even his scar began and ended exactly where it did on his cheek.

Someone knew him very, very well. And wanted him badly enough to go to the expense of printing up a reward notice.

He resisted the temptation to crumple the paper and toss it on the floor. He didn't want someone to pick it up, notice him, and decide the hundred-pound reward was worth the effort of trying to capture him. Such an action would interfere with his plans.

"Many a man would be tempted to turn ye in fer the reward," Ferret said, as though reading James's mind.

James lifted his gaze from the reward notice. "Are you tempted, Ferret?"

"'Course not. Yer me mate. Saved me life, ye did." Ferret grabbed his tankard and quickly gulped the contents. He swiped the back of his hand across his mouth. "I owe ye."

But no other man owed him. And Ferret was right. Many a man would be tempted. He thought of the barmaid's statement earlier, about him looking familiar. He wondered if she'd seen one of the reward notices. How many others might have?

With a reward on his head, he had to get out of Nouvelle-Orléans . . . and fast. But how he was going to accomplish that little miracle remained a mystery.

"I found us a cap'n who's willin' to take on a couple of experienced sea rovers like us."

James studied him. "Even a one-armed sea rover?"

"Hey! I only need one arm to cook, matey!"

"Interesting," James muttered. "You couldn't cook before."

"So I'll be apprenticin'. Ye interested in servin' as a crewman or not?" He leaned nearer and whispered. "The cap'n be askin' no questions."

"I assume the ship isn't used for legal activities," James stated.

"If he ain't askin' questions of us, I didn't feel the need to ask 'em of him."

And James had long since lost the luxury of being particular about where he berthed.

"When does he leave?"

"First light. With the morning tide."

"Sounds like our luck is improving."

"Let's finish our drinks, mate, and I'll take you to the ship and introduce you to the cap'n."

James clanked his tankard against Ferret's. "To fair winds and a fast ship."

Ferret grinned. His front teeth crossed, making him look every bit like the creature he'd been named for. "And a bit of piratin' along the way."

There was no reason to delay, so James drained his tankard in one long, hearty swallow. But Ferret still finished his first.

Neither of them had a need to return to

the squalor where they'd been living these past few weeks. James carried everything of importance on him. His pistol was tucked in his belt. His cutlass swung loosely at his side. The only clothes he owned were those on his back. He relished the freedom that his nomadic life offered him.

But sometimes he did find himself wishing for something with more permanence to it. A ship to call his own. A ship that was his to command. That would give him a place that was his. The right ship. A seaworthy ship.

He could almost see it as he wended his way through the drunken crowd, with Ferret following along behind him. But a ship cost a good deal of money.

He and Ferret stepped out into the night. The thick fog had rolled into the city. The gray mist swirled at their feet as they wandered farther away from the tavern, working their way along the narrow streets. Lanterns hung here and there created an eeriness in the fog-shrouded night.

It was nearly midnight and few people were out. Most remained in the taverns. Ferret was leading the way now.

"This way, mate."

He turned into a dark passage, buildings on either side of it. No lanterns provided light here, but farther down a glow fought the mist. It was exactly the type of place that James would use if he wanted to rob a man.

"Yo, ho, ho and a bottle —" Ferret began singing.

"Be quiet!" James commanded in a harsh whisper.

Ferret obeyed with a muttered, "Just 'avin' a bit of fun."

James crept cautiously behind Ferret. He'd never been afraid of the dark, but there was always the danger of tripping over something he couldn't see. Perhaps it was because he was concentrating so hard on his surroundings that he heard it.

A whisper of a sound.

Something that didn't belong.

The air filled with the rasp of his sword as he drew it from its sheath.

Ferret stopped. "Here now, mate. No need for that."

James could see Ferret's silhouette, the light beyond him. "Something's not right."

He felt it in his bones. The hairs along the nape of his neck prickled and rose.

"Mate, you can't —"

Ferret released a little screech and disappeared into the blackness. James heard metal scraping against metal. Light flared to the side.

He swung around. A half-dozen men stood behind him. One held a lantern aloft. Obviously, he'd had it encased in some sort of metal container to prevent it from being seen earlier.

James heard another sound and glanced over his shoulder. More light. More men.

He drew his knife from its scabbard, so he held a weapon in each hand.

A man stepped forward. "Drop your weapons, Sterling, and you'll not be harmed."

James laughed as though he were on the deck of a ship, being taunted by a bully. "If you want them, come and take them."

He arced the sword through the air, slicing nothing except fog, but it made a whistling sound that echoed between the buildings. A warning. A dare. A challenge.

He heard the rush of footsteps behind him. He swung around. His sword hit another, the ringing of steel vibrating around him. He thrust with his knife and his opponent jumped back.

James was at a disadvantage. He knew it.

There were too many. There was no escape. But he wasn't going down without a fight.

"You can't win against us," the man who'd spoken before said. "Surrender to the captain of *The Dangerous Lady*."

James spun around. "Never. I'll never surrender to you."

"I'm not the captain," the man said.

"Is he too much of a coward to do his own work?" James asked with a sneer.

A pain shot through James's head, and he dropped to his knees. Someone had sneaked up behind him and clobbered his skull. His weapons were torn from his grasp. He felt weak and the world was spinning. He tried to get up, but the ground was so much more inviting. All he wanted to do was lie down and sleep.

Someone jerked him roughly to his feet and wrenched his arms behind his back. He felt the sharp bite of rope as his hands were bound.

He heard the enticing clinking of coins. He watched, stunned, while the man who'd spoken earlier tossed a small bag into Ferret's waiting hands.

Ferret walked up to James. "Sorry, mate, but ye owed me fer takin' me arm."

Ferret took a swing, his fist clipping James on the chin and dropping him back to the ground.

"That's enough!" a feminine voice shouted.

As awkward as it was with his hands tied behind his back, James lifted his head and watched the girl walking out of the mist.

With brown hair flowing past her shoulders.

She stopped only a few inches from him.

"So we meet again, James Sterling."

It was the girl from the hold.

And from the look on her face, she had every intention of sending him to hell.

# CHAPTER TWO

Annalisa Townsend sat at the desk in her cabin. She could hardly believe that she had finally captured James Sterling.

It had been almost too easy. That thought nagged at her. She'd ordered *The Dangerous Lady* to set sail as soon as she and her men had boarded the ship — with their captive in tow.

She'd learned a lot in the year since the attack on the *Horizon*. If pirates sought to seize her ship today, she wouldn't seek refuge in the cargo hold. She'd draw her cutlass and fight the pirates. She was no longer weak and helpless. She was skilled with the parry and the thrust. She'd spent countless hours practicing, learning the techniques required to fight in close quarters aboard a ship. There was little room to maneuver, but her slender figure worked to her advantage. She was generally more nimble than her opponent, who was usually Nathaniel Northrup.

During most of the past year, she'd been under his tutelage. The young officer who'd helped her disembark from the *Horizon* had left the king's service shortly after the attack. Like her, he felt he could better serve his country as a free agent, untethered by the rules that applied to the Royal Navy. Together, they plotted and planned how best to regain what they had lost.

With money her father had set aside to be used as a dowry when she married, Annalisa had purchased an aging ship and renamed it *The Dangerous Lady*.

She wanted nothing more than to capture Crimson Kelly and regain the treasure stolen from her father. When the pirate had burned their ship and left them adrift, it had taken them some time to make it to a port where they could report the thievery. There, they'd boarded a ship that took them to New Providence. The royal governor there, Rogers, suspected her father of being in league with Crimson Kelly. Why else had the pirate not killed them all? He arrested her father and charged him with piracy!

Annalisa had pleaded with Rogers to grant her a letter of marque, to give her the chance to sail on a ship and prove her father's innocence. Rogers had merely laughed at the notion of a woman serving as a privateer. So she'd forged a marque. She needed it to declare her legitimacy at ports and to secure her crew. Otherwise, she would appear to be no more than a pirate herself — and at the mercy of other privateers.

Nathaniel had agreed to serve on Annalisa's ship as quartermaster. As such, he was the second in command. When the treasure was returned, the ship would be his, his payment for his services. He'd helped her obtain a crew. And he'd instructed her in the art of fighting with the cutlass. He'd taught her how to fire a pistol with fair accuracy. She had two loaded pistols nestled in the belt at her waist. Her sword was at the ready, at her side, along with her dagger. She'd tucked a more slender dagger into her boot.

All along the Caribbean and the coast of colonial America, Annalisa had sent her men into various taverns and pubs to gather information and post reward notices. Pirates sometimes left one ship, hoping to find work on another. With enough grog in them, they'd sell their mothers, wives, and children.

She'd managed to learn that Crimson Kelly was in the habit of burying his treasure shortly after he gained it. He favored an island in the Caribbean for his purposes, which included hiding himself between voyages. But no one knew exactly where the island was located. He shared his maps, his coordinates, with no man.

But what cabin boy didn't have a healthy dose of curiosity?

And James Sterling, if the rumors were true, had begun his pirating ways by serving as Crimson Kelly's cabin boy.

"You caught him. Shouldn't you be smiling?"

Annalisa looked up and met Nathaniel's brown-eyed gaze. With his fingers, he brushed his blond hair off his brow. He was only twenty-five, fairly young to be the quartermaster of a ship. But he had an overall sense of justice that rivaled hers. When he spoke, the crew listened. With him standing by her side, they listened when she spoke as well.

"I fear capturing him was the easy part," Annalisa said. "Getting him to cooperate is another matter."

"Are you so certain he has the answers?"

Annalisa nodded. Since she began her quest to recover the treasure stolen from her father's ship, she'd learned a great deal about Crimson Kelly and James Sterling.

"They say he was closer to Crimson Kelly than any man. That Crimson treated him almost like a son."

"Odd, then, that he would maroon him."

"He obviously fell into disfavor." She waited a heartbeat before continuing. "And that might work to our favor."

"You think he'll want his own revenge?"

"Wouldn't you?"

"Absolutely. But would I trust others to help me acquire it? I'm not sure I would."

"We'll give him no choice."

"I'm not certain why you were so determined to catch James Sterling when capturing Crimson Kelly would give us what we need."

"My reasons are personal, but I assure you they're justified. And in the end, our present course will give us much more satisfactory results."

Her comment was met with silence. As much as he questioned her, he also respected her opinion. Her plan involved finding Crimson Kelly and capturing his ship in order to reclaim the treasure. She knew — they all knew — Crimson Kelly wouldn't surrender without a ferocious fight. But it wasn't the treasure she really wanted. She wanted to free her father from suspicion, give him back his life. To achieve that end, she needed not only to recover the treasure but to deliver Crimson Kelly — alive — to Governor Rogers.

She shoved back her chair and stood. "I need to talk to our captive."

Nathaniel came to his feet. "I'll go with you."

"No, I think it best if I talk to him alone."

"That's hardly a wise plan. It puts your life at risk."

"He's in irons and caged. He can't harm me."

"It's not his hurting you that concerns me. It's his charming you."

She couldn't help herself. She laughed. "I despise the very air he breathes. He's a pirate!"

"With a reputation among the ladies. I daresay most of the information we gathered on him came from women he'd trifled with."

I promise you, Nathaniel. His charms will have no effect upon me."

She repeated those words as she stood at the top of the steps leading down to the brig. He wouldn't charm her. She'd almost forgotten what his kiss tasted like, felt like. She only remembered it when she drifted into dreams. Then it became so vivid, so real. To her mortification, she always felt a little thrill. Her life had been filled with gentlemen of the finest quality. James Sterling was like none of them. He was unpolished. A diamond in the rough. A scoundrel. A pirate.

He was the key to returning her father to her.

Holding the lantern high, she carefully descended the narrow steps. They creaked beneath her weight. She heard something scurry. A rat. How was it that they always managed to find their way aboard ships?

The dankness of the brig rose up to assail her nostrils. The flame in the lantern chased away the shadows until she spotted James Sterling squinting up at her from where he sat on the floor in the corner of his cell. There were no luxuries here. Men kept in the brig didn't deserve them.

He regarded her with insolence. The mouth he'd once pressed against hers wasn't quite smiling, not quite sneering. His flowing white shirt had seen better days. His unscarred cheek was bruised. He still wore a gold ring through his left earlobe. She'd never known another man to wear an earring. It made him seem all the more wicked. Made her heart hammer all the harder.

She cleared her throat quietly before barking out, "James Sterling."

He grinned. "You have me at a disadvantage, lass. I don't know your name."

"Annalisa Townsend. You may call me Captain Townsend."

He unfolded his body like a predator preparing to strike. In a smooth motion, he wrapped his hands around the bars and brought himself to his feet, towering over her by at least a foot. She didn't recall him being that tall.

"So formal," he fairly purred, "after we've been so . . . intimate."

"We weren't intimate."

"You taste of strawberries. How many lads know that?"

She wanted to slap him. Instead, she could

only curse the bars for being in the way, while at the same time being grateful they were. Her bravado was faltering. Facing him in person was much more disconcerting than she'd thought it would be.

"You stole that kiss and my ring. I'll have it back."

His grin widened. "By all means, I'd be more than delighted to return the kiss."

She scowled at him. "I meant the ring, you insolent dog."

He held up his left hand, examined it, studying the ring that circled the smallest finger. He took a step back. "If you want it, come and get it."

He seemed to anticipate the challenge far too much. Did he truly think she'd enter the cell? She'd not give him the satisfaction.

She waved his suggestion away. "I've decided you can keep it. It's worthless anyway."

"So I learned."

She didn't know what she expected of him. A little less cockiness. A little fear perhaps. Maybe he didn't realize exactly what was going on here — or what she wanted him to think was going on. Her marque was *forged*, after all. Not even Nathaniel knew that. But it had been the only way to give the appearance of legitimacy and get a crew to follow and respect her. Desperation required desperate acts. And lies.

"Are you familiar with New Providence?" she asked.

He simply looked at her.

"It's in the Bahamas," she explained, her impatience with him growing.

"I know where it is. I've sailed these seas a good many years."

"I plan to transport you there."

"I appreciate the offer, but I'm not interested."

"It's not an offer. It's a promise. I take it you're familiar with the reputation of its royal governor."

"I understand he is a man who possesses little humor."

He was attempting to goad her with his nonchalance. She had no plans to be goaded. But her temper was becoming sorely pricked.

"The king has charged him with ridding the area of pirates. Governor Rogers has the power to try, convict, and execute. He has exercised that power quite frequently of late."

"His mum must be proud."

"You're not taking your situation seriously, Mr. Sterling. I intend to deliver you there to stand trial. I shall serve as a witness against your evil deeds, as shall Mr. Northrup. The outcome is inevitable. You'll no doubt be found guilty of piracy."

"No doubt."

"You'll find yourself dancing the devil's jig on the gallows."

"I've never been much for dancing."

She wondered if he realized exactly what she was saying. On the one hand he seemed intelligent, on the other . . . well, he was stupid enough to become involved with pirating.

"You'll be hanged," she stated sternly.

"A rather ghastly way to go, I suspect."

"Indeed. It is not pretty, nor is it pleasant." Not that she'd ever actually witnessed a hanging, but she had a vivid imagination.

She gave all that she'd said a moment to sink in, to let him ponder the ramifications of the life he'd led and the destination to which he was sure to arrive.

She cleared her throat. "I have the power to grant you your freedom."

He cocked his head to the side, his eyes

narrowing as he studied her. It was evident he didn't quite trust her. He was smarter than he looked.

"You went to a great deal of trouble and expense to capture me. Why offer me my freedom?"

"I'm not offering you your freedom, but I'm willing to trade you for it."

He stepped nearer to the bars, his cocky grin back in place. "My freedom for a kiss?"

"You vastly overestimate your charms. Freedom for information — as long as that information bears fruit."

He narrowed his eyes again. "What information?"

"The whereabouts of the island where Crimson Kelly buries his treasure."

"Even if you found the island, you'd not find the treasure. Have you not heard how he secures his secrets? By blinding those who help him bury it, leaving them to roam over the island for the rest of their days. They say that when you get near enough to the island you can hear their souls weeping in misery."

Annalisa shuddered with the thought. She shored up her resolve to get through this encounter without revealing any squeamishness.

"If I can find the island, I can capture Crimson Kelly there when he returns to it. I'll force him to tell me where he buried the treasure."

"It's in the Bahamas. Now set me free."

He rattled the door, and she despised that the unexpected action startled her. She was striving to be the one in control. Being so easily undone was not a good sign. Touching her mother's necklace, she gathered courage.

"The Bahamas is a vast area, with more than a hundred uncharted islands. I need more information than that. I need coordinates, longitude and latitude. I need a precise location."

"Surely you jest."

"I assure you, Mr. Sterling, on the matter of the treasure entrusted to my father, I never jest."

"I can't help you. Crimson Kelly would have my head on a silver platter and my blood poured into his golden goblet."

"Are you afraid of him?" she taunted.

He laughed. "I fear no man . . . or woman."

"Then help me find him."

"In exchange for my freedom?"

"Yes. I promise you that you will be set free."

He barked out his laughter, the sound echoing between the planks. When his laughter quieted, he slowly let his gaze roam over her, as though he were measuring her worth.

"Do you think me a fool?" he asked. "A promise is easily given. I've never known one yet to be kept."

"I'll keep mine. You have my word on it."

"Your *word*?" He looked to the rafters, then slowly turned in a circle. "Where is it? I don't see it. It has no substance."

"Many a thing with substance can't be seen."

"And I trust nary a one of them. The same as I don't trust you."

The frustration ate at her. How could she convince him? "I owe you. You didn't kill me or take me captive when you had the chance. I'll return the favor now, but you must help me find Crimson Kelly."

"Ferret owed me his life as well, yet he struck a bargain with you quickly enough. You'll do the same when a better offer comes along."

"I won't. I swear —"

"Save your swearin'. I have no interest

in promises. Nor have I an interest in helping you."

"When we reach New Providence it'll be too late."

He scoffed. "Like I said. I'm not a fool. It's already too late."

"I'll give you twenty-four hours to reconsider. At that time, we'll decide whether to set course for New Providence or elsewhere."

He did nothing more than stare at her. Insolent bastard. When she could no longer stand to look at him, she spun on her heel.

"Princess?"

She looked back at him. "I'm not a princess."

"But you act like one, as though the world is yours to command, and I was put on this earth for no other purpose than to do your bidding."

"I can't deny that I consider you beneath me. If I were a boy, I'd spit on you."

"If you were a boy, I'd have taken your life in the hold."

A shiver went through her at the utter conviction of his words.

"Is nothing of value to you?" she asked.

"Precious little." He jerked his head toward her. "Don't suppose you'd leave the lantern."

"Afraid of the dark?" she taunted, loathing

**44**

him more with each passing moment. Had she really thought she had the power to convince him to help her?

"Not fond of the rats. The light keeps them at bay."

She should leave him in the dark, with the rats. He'd come around more quickly if she did. But she wasn't as ruthless as he was. Didn't want to become like him.

She hooked the lantern on a peg near the cell. With one last look at him, she turned and made her way out of the hold. He'd cooperate with her one way or another. If she had to take a cat-o'-nine-tails to his back, he'd cooperate.

James waited until the door above banged shut. Then he slid down to the floor and awkwardly brought his chained feet closer to his chained wrists. Embedded in the heel of his leather boot was a slender wire, something he kept on hand for emergencies. He'd always known capture was a possibility. He believed in being prepared for anything. Although a few things tonight had certainly taken him by surprise.

He wasn't limber enough to reach the wire

with his teeth, so he used his fingernails to work it free. When he finally had it in hand, he inserted it into the lock on the manacle of his left wrist. He dug it around, listening as the tumblers clinked, right before the manacle snapped open. He quickly opened the other one. If he heard anyone coming, he could put them back on easily enough.

Rubbing his chafed wrists, he glanced around now that he had a bit of light. Wasn't much to see. A brig was a brig. He could tell by the constant creaking of the ship and its rolling motion that they'd set sail. That surprised him. It seemed he was the only cargo they'd meant to pick up.

The girl coming to see him had taken him off guard. Her offer even more so.

He wasn't the one she was really after. She wanted Crimson.

It seemed they had a common goal in that, at least.

But he didn't trust her any more than she trusted him. Grant him his freedom? Not bloody likely.

But that didn't mean that he couldn't obtain it. On his own terms.

*     *     *

Annalisa stood at the prow, staring into the night. It was so incredibly dark on the sea. Sometimes she felt as though it could swallow her whole.

"What did he say?" Nathaniel asked quietly beside her.

She sighed deeply. "He refuses to help. I've given him twenty-four hours to reconsider."

"And if he still refuses?"

"We'll take him to New Providence, and then I suppose we shall have to redouble our efforts to find Crimson Kelly on the high seas."

"I suppose we could start the rumor that we have treasure on board. Bring the pirate to us."

She'd considered that but dismissed it as too dangerous.

"He's ruthless, Nathaniel. Better we be the ones doing the attacking."

"As you wish, Captain."

She glanced over at him. "Will you rename the ship when she's yours?"

"I will. I shall rename her *Annalisa*."

"That's hardly a name that will strike fear into the hearts of pirates."

"I care little for their hearts. I care only for yours."

Suddenly uncomfortable with the direction of the conversation, she looked back out to sea. She liked Nathaniel. She was able to breathe normally around him. She didn't grow warm. Her heart didn't pound. Her lips didn't tingle. Her knees didn't grow weak.

She turned back to Nathaniel. "I think I shall retire. Tomorrow will be a long day."

"Good night, Anna."

She left him there and made her way to her cabin. She removed her clothes and slipped on her nightgown before climbing into her bunk.

Now that she had captured James Sterling, perhaps at long last she would finally drift into sleep without dreaming about him.

# CHAPTER THREE

*Wearing a blue ball gown, Annalisa crept through the shadowy passageway. At its end was a door. Around its edges was an unnatural glow. That eerie light prevented her from being immersed in total blackness.*

*The hallway was ominously silent. No sound whatsoever.*

*Fog swirled at her feet. A chill swept through her as she reached for the door handle. She pressed it. While she heard no click, she knew she'd unlatched the door. She pushed. It opened, beckoning her in.*

*She stepped through the portal. Her breath caught. Gold. Mounds and mounds of gold, diamonds, emeralds. All spilled at her feet. It sparkled and glittered. Almost blinding her.*

*Then she saw the most beautiful necklace she'd ever seen. A dozen rubies formed a triangle. She picked it up and secured it around her throat. The red stones lay warm against her chest.*

*She turned. There was a gilt-framed looking glass. Her gown was low, her shoulders bare. The necklace was gorgeous, with nothing to detract from its beauty.*

*A slap echoed around her. Crimson flowed from one of the rubies.*

*Another slap. Another ruby wept and blood trailed over her skin.*

*Another resounding slap —*

Annalisa jerked awake. She pressed her hand to her throat. The only necklace she wore was the one her mother had always worn.

Another slap, muffled by her quarters, sounded.

But she was awake now. The slaps were real.

She clambered out of her bunk and grabbed her wrap. She was the only woman on board a ship full of men, most of them young. When she was above deck, she wore a plain brown dress that left her curves a mystery. Her belt held a light sword and a pistol. Nestled inside her boot was a dagger. She wore her hair in a single braid down her back. The breeze usually worked a few tendrils loose, but not so much that it became bothersome. A ship was not a London ballroom. She dressed appropriately, so she could move about unencumbered and swiftly.

She'd made it a rule never to run about the ship unless she was properly dressed, but she knew she didn't have time to worry over such things at the moment.

Another slap filled the air.

It was the only noise on the ship — and that's what had her tearing out of her quarters. The unnatural silence. As though no man worked. As though no man was even aboard.

She burst through the door that led onto the quarterdeck. Since it was one level up from the main deck, she had a good view of most of the ship. At the far end, men were gathered in a large cluster, but she could see over their heads.

She could see the man with his arms raised high, his wrists tied to the foremast. She could see one of the crewmen, the burliest of the lot — Kane — holding the cat-o'-nine-tails, bringing it back, flicking it forward.

"No!" she shouted.

But he had his momentum, and the nine writhing lashes with their metal tips slapped against James Sterling's bare back. The man hardly flinched.

"Stop it!" she shouted repeatedly with each step she took as she pushed and shoved her way through the men, trying to reach the middle of the ship.

When she finally made her way to the front of the gathering, Kane stood there breathing heavily, the tips of his whip having left a bloody trail against the planked flooring.

Her pirate had his eyes squeezed shut, his jaw clenched, his hands balled into white-knuckled fists. But he made no sound. If it weren't for the shallow rising and falling of his chest, she'd have thought he was dead.

"Anna, it's best if you not interfere."

It was only then that she noticed Nathaniel standing to the side, his hands behind his back. How could he appear so utterly calm, as though he was merely waiting for tea to finish steeping?

"Why are you doing this?" she asked.

"Sterling refuses to help us. He'll begin each day with a dozen lashes until he is broken —"

"No!"

He took a step nearer to her, a hardness in his eyes that she'd never before seen. "Anna, you have too gentle a heart for what is needed. So now he shall deal with me."

"I'm captain of this ship. I forbid flogging."

"Don't be rash. It's a common practice to give a man who is disobedient a taste of the cat. Take away that punishment and you'll have to find another to keep the men in line, lest ye have a mutiny on your hands."

"I'd think you'd have a mutiny if you went about flogging them."

Nathaniel looked past her. "You men are dismissed. Get back about your duties!" He returned his attention to her. "You are captain because it is your ship, not because you have the experience to lead."

"This is not leading. This is bullying."

She spun around to find Kane still standing there. She snatched the whip from his hand, marched to the side of the ship, and tossed it into the murky depths of the ocean.

She stormed back to the mast and addressed Kane. "Cut Sterling down immediately and carry him to my quarters. Then fetch the physician."

Kane touched his fingers to his brow. "Aye, Cap'n."

He pulled his knife free and went about cutting the bindings that held Sterling secure. Annalisa felt tears sting her eyes at the sight of poor Sterling's bloodied back. She heard him muffle a moan, obviously trying not to let on how badly he'd been hurt.

"You're not going to have him in your quarters dressed like that, are you?" Nathaniel asked, clear disapproval in his voice.

"I doubt he'd be able to stand wearing a shirt, at least not until the doctor's tended to his wounds."

"I wasn't referring to his clothing but yours."

Only then did she remember that she'd come straight from bed. She turned to face him. "I can't believe you did this."

"I know how important finding Crimson Kelly is to you. I did this for you."

"Gentlemen generally give flowers to a lady when they wish to earn her favor."

He gave her a sad smile. "Flowers are bad luck aboard ship. Considered to be an omen of deaths to come. Perhaps when we return to shore . . ."

She shook her head. He was missing her point entirely. "Sterling can't be broken."

"Every man can be broken."

She glared at him, at the ruthlessness of his words. So unlike him. While she knew he was brave and strong and determined, he'd never been cruel. The crew liked him because he treated them all fairly. She liked him because he believed in justice — as she did.

"You act as though I'm the villain here," Nathaniel said. "Yes, it was brutal, but brutality is all he understands. I didn't think you'd object."

"Then why do it while I was asleep?"

"Because neither did I think you'd have the stomach for it." He took her hand. "I suspect most of the men have been flogged at one time or another. It's part of life at sea."

"Not aboard my ship. Is that understood?"

His jaw tightened, his eyes hardened, and she expected him to object. Instead, he merely gave a brusque nod and touched his fingers to his brow in salute. "Aye, aye, Captain."

"Thank you, Nathaniel. I depend upon your wisdom, your knowledge, and your dedication to righteousness. You are a man of honor.

Please don't lose that in our quest to recover what we lost."

"Pirates are a blight upon this earth."

"I don't disagree, but neither should we stoop to their level."

"Haven't we already, Anna?"

She shook her head, refusing to acknowledge that she was closer to being a pirate than she cared to admit. "No, we have not."

When she returned to her cabin, Dr. Gabriel was already there examining Sterling's back. Sterling lay on his stomach, on her bunk, his eyes closed. She wondered if he was sleeping. She doubted it. He was probably unconscious. Or perhaps he'd closed his eyes in order to hide what he was feeling.

"How badly is he hurt?" she asked the doctor.

"Could have been worse," Dr. Gabriel said as he dabbed a cloth against the cuts.

Sterling flinched ever so slightly.

"My apologies," Dr. Gabriel said. "I'm going to clean the cuts, put some salve on your wounds. Bandage them up. I'm surprised by the condition of your back. It doesn't appear you've been flogged before."

"Pirates don't flog," Sterling said between clenched teeth.

"Truly?" Annalisa asked.

Sterling peered at her through narrowed eyes. "Hardly ever."

It looked as though he wanted to say more. Instead, he slammed his eyes closed and hissed with a sharp intake of breath as Dr. Gabriel continued his ministrations.

Watching his suffering, it was difficult to remember he was a pirate and no doubt deserving of such treatment. If only he'd agreed to help her, he'd have been spared.

Still, she couldn't find it within herself to blame Nathaniel. After all, she'd toyed with the notion of taking a lash to Sterling's back. How could she remain angry at her quartermaster for actually carrying through on something she'd considered? The difference, she supposed, was that even as she'd thought it, she'd known she'd never give the order to carry out the punishment.

Her world had been turned upside down when the pirates had attacked. Her innocence had been shattered. She despised them. Despised them all.

Despised James Sterling most of all.

Because even now, she longed to be kissed by him once again.


Annalisa Townsend had very nice ankles.

If he were a gentleman, James wouldn't look. But then he'd never claimed to be a gentleman. Quite the opposite, in fact. He'd always admitted to being exactly what he was: a rogue, a scoundrel, a pirate.

And any pirate worth his salt would steal a peek at Miss Townsend's ankles.

After the doctor left, she'd moved a screen into place and gone behind it to change her clothes. Obviously, she'd assumed he was either asleep or unconscious. Otherwise, she'd not have done something so daring.

But his back felt as though fiery flames licked at it. It would be a good long while before he found solace in sleep.

The screen stood on spindly legs, the bottom open, giving him a clear view. And so he watched her feet, her ankles, a bit of her calves as she went about dressing herself. From time to time, she would place one small, slender foot on top of the other. After a while, her hands appeared over the top of the screen as she wiggled into her dress.

When she came out from behind the screen, she walked to the bunk and stared down at him. He'd closed his eyes, surprised to discover that even though he couldn't see her, he was acutely aware of her presence. When she moved away, he peered through his lashes and watched as she sat in a chair at the table and slipped on her stockings, then her boots.

She turned her head slightly and looked at him. He knew he still appeared to be asleep, because she didn't seem at all concerned. He wondered what she was thinking. What did she see when she looked at him? Did she think badly of him?

Of course she did. He was idiotic to think otherwise. Why did he care that she wouldn't think favorably of him? He didn't care at all.

A knock sounded on the door. She popped up from her chair, smoothed her skirt as though needing time to gather herself. "Enter."

The door opened and a seaman walked in. "Yer breakfast, Cap'n."

Carefully, he balanced a tray, his stomach serving as an anchor since he had only one arm. Ferret!

"Bloody hell! What are you doing here?" James demanded, coming upright and grimacing as pain knifed through his back.

Screeching like a mouse cornered by a cat, Ferret dropped the tray and skittered back.

Anna spun around, the wrath of a thousand women scorned evident in her face. "How long have you been awake?"

"Long enough." Groaning, he swung his legs off the bunk.

Her second in command crashed through the door, his sword drawn. Always the knight in shining armor. Disgustingly so. James found himself wondering if he'd kissed Anna, if she'd kissed him back willingly. Had she freely given to Northup what James had been reduced to stealing from her?

"What's amiss here?" Northrup said, his voice full of authority.

"Nothing," Anna said, clearly exasperated.

"I didn't know he be out and about. I thought he be in the brig," Ferret said.

"He should be," Northrup said. "You!" He pointed his sword at James. "On your feet. Handsomely now!"

"No," Anna said. "He's still bleeding. He'll

stay here through the day. Less chance of infection."

"And more chance of his causing mischief."

"He's hardly in a condition to get into mischief." She nodded at Ferret. "Clean this up and bring some more."

"Aye, Cap'n." Ferret made quick work of cleaning up what appeared to be porridge. Since it had been in a wooden bowl nothing had broken, so he was spared that mess.

Everyone was quiet while he worked. No one quite trusted him not to repeat what might be said in the captain's quarters. When he finally left, Northrup said, "Anna, you can't keep Sterling here. The men will talk. Your reputation —"

"Went to the devil the day I decided to captain a ship." Looking none too pleased, she walked over to James. "Lie back down so I can see if you undid the good doctor's work."

Biting back a moan, he did as she ordered. He wasn't a fool. Her bunk was preferable to the brig.

Her fingers touched his shoulder. They were so warm, so gentle. "I think you're all right."

She backed up a step.

"You and I have a different understanding of all right," he grumbled.

"I simply meant that I don't think I need to send for the doctor again."

She strode to her desk and sat in a large leather chair behind it. She opened a journal, dipped her quill into the ink pot, and began to write. "Since Mr. Sterling has declined to help us, we have no cause to delay. We'll set a course for the Bahamas. See to it, Mr. Northrup."

"You shouldn't be alone with the likes of him."

"I have two pistols, a sword, and a knife. Quite honestly, I've lost patience and would welcome an excuse to use one or all on him. So see to your duties and I shall see to mine."

James could almost feel the bite of the cat-o'-nine in the glare that Northrup gave him.

"Aye, Captain, but I'll leave the door open," Northrup finally said before turning on his heel and storming from the room.

"Right jolly fellow there," James muttered.

"Like me, Mr. Sterling, he has little patience with pirates. I suggest you rest and gather your strength. You'll need it to fight off the rats in the brig."

She tried valiantly to be tough, but he'd seen the tears in her eyes when the doctor had been tending his back.

"Why do you want Crimson so badly?" he asked.

"For the same reason I wanted you. He stole from me."

"You've made it very personal."

She came up out of the chair with the force of the wrath of an avenging angel. "It is personal. The treasure belonged to the king. My father was responsible for it. Now he sits in prison at New Providence, under suspicion of piracy or cowardice — Rogers has not yet determined which — because my father survived."

"And now you risk your life to save his?"

"He knows nothing of what I'm doing, and I'll not have you call it into question. It's enough for you to know I want the treasure."

With a flounce, she turned on her heel, walked back to her desk, and sat in her chair. Very deliberately, she dipped her quill into the inkwell and began scratching in her journal.

"What were you doing on the *Horizon*?" he asked.

Her hand stilled, her quill poised above the

paper. "At the behest of the king, my father was to serve as the royal governor of Mourning. Do you know the island?"

"Aye." He narrowed his eyes. "It doesn't even have a decent port."

"The reason the king sent gold with my father. So one could be built."

"And you think returning the treasure —"

"Will give the governor no reason to hold him." She gave him a hard look. "Not to mention the justice of it, which I'm fairly certain you're unable to comprehend. Pirates do not have a right to steal."

"So you want to put an end to pirating?"

"I do. I never want anyone to experience the terror I did that morning when the *Phantom Mist* attacked us."

He refused to allow her words to make him feel guilty. "I didn't harm you."

"You threatened me, Mr. Sterling. You stole my ring."

He felt it grow warm on his finger. He was surprised she'd not taken it when she had the chance.

"I was merely carrying on a tradition that began when men first began to travel the seas."

"Thievery?"

"There have always been pirates, m'lady."

She straightened in her chair. "And there have always been those willing to challenge them."

She was so easily angered. So righteous. He couldn't deny that he enjoyed pricking her temper.

A knock sounded on the door. "Enter."

James was expecting Ferret, returning with his porridge. Instead, it was the bloke who'd wielded the lash.

"Cap'n, Mr. Northrup sent me to fetch you. There's something he needs you to see."

"Thank you, Mr. Kane." She rose from the chair and walked to the door.

James couldn't believe his luck. He was going to be left alone.

"Mr. Kane, please escort Mr. Sterling back to the brig."

"Aye, aye, Cap'n."

Kane walked into the room. He was a huge bulk of a man. James could see two swords, the hilt of two knives, and three pistols strapped across the man's chest.

"Don't be giving me any trouble, pirate."

James slowly, laboriously made his way out of the bunk. "Wouldn't dream of it, mate."

# CHAPTER FOUR

Annalisa joined Nathaniel at the prow of the ship. "You wished to see me, Mr. Northup?"

"Yes, Captain," he said most formally.

He pointed toward the east. "It looks like we might be headed into a storm. Do you want to stay on this course?"

In the distance the clouds were black and low. It almost looked as though they were touching the water.

She suspected Nathaniel was feeling wounded from their earlier encounter when she'd questioned his judgment. Now she asked, "What do you recommend?"

His gaze darted to her quickly, before he turned his attention back to the sea. "It'll be rough sailing for a bit, no doubt about that.

But the ship is seaworthy. She can take it. Staying on course will get us to the Bahamas sooner, and we'll have one less pirate to worry over."

"Perhaps we should trim the sails a bit, though. No sense in rushing headlong into a storm, but I agree we should stay on course."

"As you wish."

"Do you think they'll hang Sterling?"

"Absolutely."

"Governor Rogers is known to grant pardons to pirates who renounce their wayward life."

"James Sterling tossed your offer for freedom back into your face. Do you not think he'll do the same to Rogers? Sterling values nothing except the clinking of coins. And even if he is granted amnesty, he'll soon be back to his pirating ways. I have no doubt he is headed toward a noose."

"You don't much like him."

Nathaniel looked at her as though he couldn't believe she'd said that. "In so short a time, he's already managed to charm you."

"No, of course he hasn't. I threatened him with hanging. You tried brutality."

He flinched.

"Perhaps we used the wrong tactic."

"And what would you recommend? Serving him tea?"

His voice contained a great deal of chiding. And she knew her next words were going to be met with resistance.

"Not tea. Dinner."

Nathaniel turned slowly and faced her completely. "You're not serious."

"He refused to help because he doesn't think I'll keep my word. If he knew me better —"

"He'll take advantage of you, Anna. He'll determine your strengths and your weaknesses and he'll prey upon them."

She angled her chin. "What weaknesses?"

"Your kind heart for one." He looked out to sea. "Treat him with all the civility you want. You can't tame him."

She wasn't certain she really wanted to.

"We need Crimson Kelly alive in order to find out where he buried the treasure, and Sterling is the only one who knows the man well enough to help us lay a trap. Even that Ferret fellow hasn't a clue as to where the island might be."

"Not surprising there. He doesn't strike me

as a man who knows much of anything. I can't believe you took him on as a cook's assistant."

"I felt I owed him more than the reward. It would hardly keep him in grog for long."

"Your generous soul will get you in trouble one day, Anna. I do hope you won't hold the actions I took this morning against me. They were well-intentioned."

She rubbed her hand up and down his arm. "I know. I suppose I worry that we could easily become what we're hunting."

He nodded slowly but kept his gaze on the approaching storm. "Very easily indeed."

How could she convince a pirate that she could be trusted? Especially James Sterling, who'd been betrayed at least twice by all accounts — first marooned by his captain, then traded for coin by his mate.

Annalisa pondered her dilemma all day as the ship slowly sailed south by southeast. The winds began to pick up as the storm seemed to turn toward them. They could possibly outrun it, but there was no way to be sure which direction would guarantee them safe haven. Better to face the devil than have him at your back.

For now the rain merely battered the ship and the swells were growing slightly angrier, but no one was overly concerned. They weren't in the midst of a full tempest, so Annalisa was continuing with her plans for dinner. Besides, they all needed to eat.

For her special guest, she'd brought out her best. She'd planned to wear the royal blue Empire style dress to her father's first dinner party as governor. But there had been no joyous celebration when he arrived at New Providence to report the attack. There'd been only fury, blame, and distrust.

They'd thrown her father in prison. He'd become a man broken in spirit and heart. Even if they didn't kill him, he now had no more life to him than a corpse. Crimson Kelly had stolen her father when he'd stolen the gold.

She'd get the treasure in order to return her father to her. But Crimson Kelly she'd see hanged.

Of course, she had to find him first. And James Sterling was the key to unlocking that door.

So tonight she wore her royal blue gown. Her hair she'd brushed to a fine sheen and left hanging loose, past her shoulders. It was thick and luxurious, her crowning glory. While she was not vain, she knew young men found her beautiful. She intended to use her beauty as a weapon against Sterling.

He'd kissed her once. He'd hinted that he wanted to kiss her again. The first kiss he'd stolen. The next one would cost him dearly.

When she was satisfied with her appearance, she stepped out of what passed as her private quarters, where her bed was nestled, into the larger part of the captain's cabin. Here was a long table with five chairs on either side and one at either end so eleven of her officers could join her for supper.

At her desk, Nathaniel often discussed their plans and their course, mapping out the route. He was the skilled seaman. By all rights, he should have the captain's cabin. But this venture was her idea, her quest. So she slept in the nicest quarters on the ship and felt only a bit of guilt about it.

Tonight she'd use it to bait Sterling into helping her.

She'd sent Nathaniel and several men to fetch the pirate. Before they brought him up, though, they were to make him take a bath and give him fresh clothes. Since he'd be sharing her meal, she didn't want the odors from the brig trailing in with him.

As she paced in front of her desk, she wondered what was taking them so long. In her experience, ladies always took longer to prepare themselves than gentlemen. Hadn't her father spent countless minutes waiting on her mother?

Surely Sterling would relish the opportunity to rid himself of the filth that had accumulated since his capture. And clean clothes were a luxury she had little doubt he'd been without for a while. He was close to Nathaniel in height. A bit taller, a bit broader across the shoulders, perhaps. But close enough that Nathaniel's clothes should fit him comfortably.

Tonight she would treat him like a civilized man instead of the barbaric pirate he was. She'd appeal to the decency that she was certain resided somewhere within his soul. She'd not think about the kiss. She'd not get angry. She'd be reasonable. And in turn, so would he.

After all, she'd used valid argument and logic to convince Nathaniel to help her. She'd apply the same approach to Sterling.

Hearing the thunderous footsteps, she

stopped her pacing, took a deep breath, and faced the door. They were bringing him to her. With any luck, before the night was done, she'd have their destination plotted and the course marked.

The knock sounded on her door so loudly that it almost vibrated through her chest.

She swallowed hard and touched her mother's necklace, gathering her resolve to portray a calm facade. "Enter."

The door opened and Nathaniel stepped in. "Captain, we've brought the prisoner as you ordered."

Silently, she thanked him for using her title and for making it clear that he followed her orders. She needed Sterling to see her not as the frightened girl in the hold but as a young woman who had control not only of this ship but of her destiny.

Two crewmen, standing on either side of Sterling, holding his arms firmly, shoved him into the room. He was still manacled, but he and his clothes were now clean. Which should have been an improvement. Should have made him look less threatening.

But her heart had started pounding and her hands had dampened while her mouth had grown dry. It seemed her body was as confused as she. How could he now appear so much more dangerous?

Why was she suddenly so unsure of her plan, terrified that it would result in disaster? Perhaps it was because she could almost forget he was a pirate. Perhaps because for one insane moment she wondered what it might be like to stroll through a moonlit garden with him, dart behind a rose-covered trellis, and rise up on her toes . . .

"Mr. Sterling, I thought you might like to join Mr. Northrup and me for dinner."

Nathaniel's eyes widened at that pronouncement because the plan had not been to include him, but suddenly Annalisa was feeling less confident. Being alone with Sterling, where no bars separated them, was probably not the wisest of moves.

He seemed to have recovered quite nicely from his earlier ordeal. She noted no stiffness in his movements as he assessed the room as though he thought he had a chance of escaping through the portal. Finally, his eyes came back to her. It irritated her that he could dismiss her far more easily than she seemed capable of dismissing him.

"I'd be honored." He bowed slightly, mockingly so. He held up his shackled wrists. "I assume we'll dispense with these bothersome encumbrances."

"No, we shan't," Nathaniel said before Annalisa could speak. He looked over at her. "We had a bit of a scuffle on the way here. I think Sterling has the notion of trying to escape."

"You can hardly hold my actions against me considering what happened the last time I was taken from the brig," Sterling said.

"Yes, you were treated quite unfairly this morning. How is your back?" Annalisa asked.

"Feel nary a thing."

She doubted that. But she also doubted he'd admit if he did.

He rattled his chains. "Now what about these?"

She looked at Nathaniel. "We're in the middle of the ocean. Where could he go?"

"Free about the ship, I think he could do a great deal of harm." He held her gaze. "To you especially."

"I've never harmed a woman in my life," Sterling said defensively.

But that didn't mean that he wouldn't.

Annalisa remembered his threats in the hold. She nodded toward Nathaniel. "You're right, of course. Sterling, have a seat."

She dismissed the two crewmen. They closed the door in their wake.

Before she could pull out her own chair, Nathaniel moved quickly to do it for her. He was always courteous, always polite. She was at an age when she should be courted, attending balls and having fun. Instead, she was suffering the hardships of the sea. She smiled at him. "Thank you, Nathaniel. If you'll do the honors . . ."

She sat, paying little attention as Sterling took his place and Nathaniel sliced and served the seasoned beef. Meals were always better at the beginning of the voyage, while the meat was fresh. Potatoes and carrots completed the offerings. When Nathaniel had filled everyone's plates, he sat. Annalisa concentrated on cutting her meat into smaller portions. She was suddenly very self-conscious that they'd kept Sterling in chains, especially as they rattled with his movements below the table. She was acutely aware that his eating would be awkward, perhaps even embarrassing for him.

She glanced up. "Would you like me to cut your meat into smaller portions?"

He grinned easily. "Yes, please."

His eagerness surprised her. As she got up and walked to the far end of the table, she felt Nathaniel's eyes on her, his disapproval evident. Sterling's shackled wrists were in his lap, hidden beneath the table. She brought his plate nearer to her and began cutting his meat into more manageable pieces. She noticed that his portion was thicker than hers, would be more difficult to handle. She wondered if Nathaniel had done it on purpose, to give Sterling no choice except to eat like a barbarian.

"You always smell so sweet," Sterling said quietly.

She was certain her face was turning red, because her cheeks felt so hot. "You smell somewhat better than you did. Did you enjoy your bath?"

"I'd have enjoyed it better without an audience."

"You can hardly blame us for not trusting you, Mr. Sterling."

"Don't blame you at all, m'lady. But if

they'd explained having a bath meant sharing a dinner with you, I might not have fought them."

She stopped slicing the meat and looked at him. "They didn't explain —"

"They said nary a word."

"My apologies, Mr. Sterling. You're our first prisoner. I'm afraid we haven't quite worked out our protocol."

"I'd be more than happy to provide suggestions."

She didn't like being this close to him, seeing the scar on his cheek, wondering how he'd come to have it. Looking into eyes as green as the sea.

"I'm sure you would."

She turned back to the task at hand, quickly finished up, and shoved his plate back into place. "There."

Before she could retreat, he grabbed her hand. She jerked back to face him. His eyes captured hers, holding her attention as he grinned. "Thanks, m'lady."

He kissed the back of her hand and winked at her. It was only then that she noticed he was no longer shackled.

A chair scraped across the floor as Nathaniel came to his feet. "See here, Sterling!"

"You're not shackled," she said lamely.

"Picked the locks. Can't stand being in chains."

She snatched her hand free of his. "And the lock to your cell door?"

"That one remains a mystery to me."

She didn't believe it. Not for one moment.

She heard a thump, and suddenly Nathaniel had Sterling by the front of his shirt, jerked him out of the chair, and slammed him against the cabin wall. She heard Sterling grunt, whether from the impact or the pressure of wood against his cuts, she did not know.

"Nathaniel!"

She moved to break them apart, only to find Nathaniel still, his eyes wide, because even though he held Sterling, Sterling pressed a pistol beneath Nathaniel's chin. Nathaniel's pistol. Sterling had no doubt snagged it when Nathaniel had pushed him against the wall.

"Tell him to back off, m'lady," Sterling ordered.

"Nathaniel, release him."

"Not until he drops the pistol."

"Then we're at a standoff, mate," Sterling said. "I'm not giving up my advantage. I'll not feel the bite of the cat again."

"We're not at a standoff," Annalisa said. "Nathaniel, I order you to release him. Sterling, I order you to lower the pistol. Both of you, on the count of three. One, two, three."

Nathaniel dropped his arms to his side. But the pistol remained beneath his chin.

"Sterling, I brought you here to offer you an opportunity to be part of this crew," Annalisa said.

He slid his gaze over to her. At least she had his interest.

"First you capture me, threaten me with hanging, then you take a cat-o'-nine to me, and now you want to make me part of your crew?"

"We need your help to find the treasure. We tried bullying you. That obviously didn't work."

"So you thought to sweeten me up?"

"I thought to approach you with a bit more civility. You can't escape. And if you shoot him, I'll give my life to see you hanged."

He seemed surprised by her response. "Do you care about him that much?"

"He's part of my crew. I care about my crew."

Without a word, he lowered the pistol, tossed it up, caught it by the barrel, and extended it toward her. She took it from him. "Thank —"

Before she could finish, Nathaniel's fist snapped Sterling's head back. His skull cracked against the wall. With a groan, he slumped to the floor.

"Nathaniel!" She scolded him fiercely before kneeling beside Sterling. She tried to convince herself that she'd show the same concern toward any man who was hurt. That the concern she was now expressing for this man was not out of the ordinary. "Are you all right?"

Sterling shoved himself into a sitting position and leaned against the wall. He pressed the back of his hand against his bleeding lower lip. "Couldn't be better."

"Let me see."

She raised her hand and he shoved it away.

"Don't touch her, you vile dog!" Nathaniel ordered.

The ship suddenly roiled. Nathaniel teetered, trying to catch his balance. Annalisa had no opportunity to catch herself before she toppled into Sterling's lap, the pistol flying from her hand to land beyond reach. Because he was braced against the wall, he was as steady as a rock, his arms strong as they came around her.

"I think I could learn to enjoy storms," he said, grinning arrogantly.

"Unhand me."

"Or what, m'lady?"

Reaching down, she snatched the knife from inside her boot and had it at his throat before he realized what she was about. She took keen satisfaction in watching his smile dim. "I'll have you flogged again."

Suddenly, the pistol was pressed against Sterling's temple. Nathaniel had apparently not only recovered from his spill but recovered the pistol as well. "Release her."

"Do you treat all your dinner guests so rudely?" Sterling asked.

"Only the thieves. Now release her."

"If he kills me, you'll never get what you want," Sterling said.

"I'll take my chances," she said.

Just as he loosened his hold, the ship

tilted again. Nathaniel staggered backward and landed with a thud on his backside, and Annalisa found herself held even more tightly. To her horror, blood trailed down Sterling's throat. She'd accidentally cut him. "Oh, dear Lord! You're bleeding!"

"Don't fret over it. I consider a bit of bloodletting a fair trade to hold you in my arms."

"Oh, you arrogant dolt!" She pressed against him. To her surprise, she came free of his hold quite easily.

The ship dipped again, and Annalisa scurried back. She heard the groaning as though the ship was protesting its treatment by the sea. "The storm's worsening."

She tucked the knife back into her boot, then scrambled to her feet. The ship lurched and she grabbed the table to steady herself and prevent her fall. It was bolted to the floor, unlike the chairs, which scattered across the planked flooring.

"We're going to have to get him back into the brig," Nathaniel said.

"Don't be daft, man," Sterling said. "You're going to need all the help you can get up top."

"You're mad if you think we're going to trust you. You'll slit our throats first chance you get."

Sterling jerked his gaze to her. "I plan to escape, but not during a storm that'll capsize a small boat. And I don't fancy being shipwrecked." He shoved against the wall, pushing himself up until he was standing. "I'm worth my salt up top."

"I'll have your word that you'll fight the storm and not us," she said.

"You can't honestly believe you can trust him," Nathaniel said.

She knew she shouldn't trust Sterling. He was, after all, a pirate. And they'd not treated him particularly well.

"Your word," she repeated. "Even though I can't see it or hold it in my hand, I do believe it is of value. If you give it to me, I shan't throw it in your face."

"You have it."

"How do you know you can trust him?" Nathaniel shouted.

"Because I can't swim, mate. I'll make my escape when the waters are calm."

She didn't have time to consider the absurdity of a pirate who couldn't swim or reflect further on the wisdom of trusting him. He'd managed to free his hands, but his ankles were still bound by the chains. "Unshackle him."

"Anna —"

"Do it!"

With a harsh breath, Nathaniel did her bidding, kneeling at Sterling's feet, key in hand. She thought she could almost read the thoughts crossing through Sterling's mind — that perhaps he could get away with kicking Nathaniel.

"Don't even consider it," she warned.

He shifted his gaze to her, grinned his devilish grin.

The shackles clanked as they hit the floor. Stepping away, Sterling opened the door, stopped, and glanced back over his shoulder. "You should stay here, m'lady."

Then he disappeared, bounding down the short hallway. A shiver went through Annalisa as she remembered the last time he'd disappeared and the terror she'd felt then. It wasn't so different from what she felt now. Only this time, she had no intention of hiding.

She hurried after him, the ship bucking like

an untamed horse. She lost her footing once, twice, but finally made it to the doorway. The wind had caught the door when Sterling went through it, holding it open as though the storm was inviting them out to play.

She watched in horror as huge swells crashed over the sides of the ship, knocking men off their feet. They scrabbled to latch onto anything that would keep them anchored.

She felt Nathaniel's presence behind her. Glancing back, she could read the hesitation in his face. He slid his gaze to her. "Stay here, Anna. The strength of the waves will wash you overboard."

"I could tie a rope —"

"Stay here! I can't save the ship if I'm worried about saving you."

He wound an arm around her waist, drew her close, bent his head, and kissed her. Hard.

Then, like James Sterling, he was gone.

To fight the storm.

She heard him shouting the order to batten down. She watched as men began hammering closed hatches. She watched as others climbed the rigging, to secure the sails. They were all risking their lives.

And she wasn't. She couldn't ask of them what she wasn't willing to do.

Stepping out onto the deck, she was immediately caught by the strong gale and smashed against the railing, the breath knocked out of her. She fell to her knees.

Struggling for breath, she glanced up and saw Sterling at the helm. The lightning flashed, outlining the concentration on his face. She looked in the direction he was gazing, and her stomach roiled as forcefully as the ocean.

A wall of water had reared up . . . and there was no escaping it!

# CHAPTER FIVE

Bloody hell, but it hurt being dead!

James didn't think there was a single part of him that wasn't in agony. Battered and bruised from head to toe. Well, maybe his little toe had been spared. He wiggled it. No, it hurt, too.

What a miserable way to spend eternity!

Although it occurred to him that the very fact that he was in pain might mean he wasn't dead after all.

He'd been at the helm, working with that jackanapes quartermaster, trying to turn the ship, when he'd seen Anna go down. And when had he begun thinking of her as Anna? Perhaps when he'd seen her ankles. It had seemed an intimacy far more personal than sharing a kiss.

But seeing her slammed into the deck of the ship, he'd known she wouldn't have the strength to hold on when the wave crashed down on them. He'd left his post and thrown himself around her, shielding her and holding on to the ropes securing the rainwater barrel to the side of the ship. He remembered the lash of the wave, as brutal as any beating he'd ever been given. And the scent of strawberries. Even in the raging storm, he'd somehow smelled her.

He smelled her still.

Felt something cool brush lightly across his brow.

Slowly, he opened his eyes.

And there she was. Wiping his brow with a look of tenderness the likes of which he'd never seen. At least not since his mother had sold him to Crimson. And why him? He'd not been the oldest of her brood. Two were older; three were younger. Nor had he been the one who ate the most. That honor had gone to his oldest brother, who'd been known to steal gruel from James's bowl when their mother wasn't looking. He'd tried to be a good son. But she'd sold him anyway.

"Sterling?"

Annalisa's soft voice prodded him back from memories he preferred keeping locked away. He was no mother's son. No father's, either. He made his way by stealth and cunning. His only dream — too sweet a word for the hunger that gnawed at him — was to be captain of his own ship. The captain took orders from no man. And while a mutiny might result in his death, until that time no one would ever beat him. He was protected from those who awoke in a foul mood.

He tried to gauge his surroundings. He seemed to be in a berth, cushioned by softness. He'd been here before.

"I seem to have found my way back into your bed." His voice sounded hoarse and his throat felt raw when he spoke.

He'd hoped for a bit of a smile. Instead, she furrowed her brow. "Here, try to drink some water."

Slipping an arm beneath his head, she raised him up a bit before placing a glass against his lips. The water soothed going down. He realized the ship was no longer rocking. The storm must have passed. It always amazed him how he could look on a sea after a storm and find no evidence of its passing. If he ever had a ship of his own, he wanted to be like the storm. Attack, then disappear. Leaving those who survived in awe, forever referring to the powerful and mighty pirate who'd had the cunning to disappear as though he'd never been there.

Annalisa moved the glass away. "How are you feeling?"

"Like I got in a fight with the devil."

She laughed lyrically. "That's as good a way to describe what we went through as anything, I suppose."

She was wearing a green dress now, instead of the blue. Her hair was pulled back, held in place with a ribbon. A bruise marred her cheek.

"You're hurt." It was difficult to tell with the scratchiness of his voice if he was asking a question or stating a fact.

"Not as badly as I might have been, if you hadn't . . ." Her voice trailed off and she looked at her hands, clasped in her lap. She was sitting in a narrow chair. This portion of the captain's cabin barely had room for that. She lifted her gaze. "You saved my life."

He was uncomfortable with the gratitude he saw in her eyes. "Don't make me out to be a hero, m'lady. I was watching out for my own skin. Your Mr. Northrup would just as soon hang me from the highest yardarm. You, on the other hand, have an interest in keeping me alive."

"That interest is dwindling, Mr. Sterling, since you refuse to help me."

Her voice was tart, and he couldn't deny that he much preferred her sparring with him. Much safer that way, easier to keep his distance. He'd loved his mum and she'd sold him. As daft as it sounded, he suspected he'd loved Crimson as well. He'd been the closest thing James had to a father. But Crimson had marooned him. All because of a piece of jewelry.

"Offer me something more valuable than my freedom."

"There is nothing more valuable than your freedom."

"Freedom I can acquire on my own. Offer me something I can't."

She shoved back her chair, stood, and crossed her arms over her chest. "You're quite arrogant, you know that?"

"It's the pirate in me."

"You are my prisoner. I hold your fate in my hands."

92

"You owe me, m'lady. Twice now." He held up two fingers to make his point. "The first time in the hold —"

"They didn't kill my father."

"And I daresay they'd not have killed you, but you'd have wished they had when they were finished with you."

She blanched, her face growing pale. He didn't know what possessed him to challenge her at every turn. He was in danger of losing what he most wanted to acquire.

"I won't tell you where Crimson is," he said, "but I'll take you to him. If I consider the trade fair."

"And what would make the trade more fair than giving you your life?"

"The quartermaster's cabin."

She blinked and slowly unfolded her arms. "Pardon?"

"I don't want to be kept in the brig, nor do I want to sleep in crowded, squalid conditions where the regular crewmen stay." He nodded, taking a fancy to the idea. "I want a comfortable berth. The quartermaster's cabin will do nicely."

"Over my dead body." Suddenly, Northrup was standing in the doorway.

James hated realizing that perhaps he'd been eavesdropping, that he'd heard everything spoken. "That can be arranged," he said cockily, only too eager to make his claim a reality.

"Enough, you two. The squabbling has to stop," Annalisa said.

"I'm the quartermaster, Anna," Northrup said. "I'll not sleep with the men. They'll lose all respect for me. I can't command without respect."

James was surprised to discover that he didn't like the way she looked at Northrup, the soft smile she gave him, the way she reached out and squeezed his hand.

"Set up a hammock in your quarters. Give him the bed. Please, Nathaniel. You know how much this means to me. And it's just for a short time."

Northrup narrowed his eyes at James. James saw his jaw tighten. He thought if they spent much time in each other's company, he'd have the quartermaster grinding his teeth down to nubs. He took perverse pleasure in the notion.

Northrup looked back at Anna, touched her cheek with a familiarity that caused James's stomach to tighten. He'd seen his mates pull wenches he'd been flirting with onto their laps, and he'd not been bothered. Why was he bothered by something passing between Anna and Northrup that seemed so . . . inconsequential?

"For you, Anna. I'll do it for you," Northrup said.

She gave him a soft smile, the type of smile James knew she'd never give to him. One of fondness, one of caring. He turned his head away. It was difficult to watch this awkward encounter between them, to realize that Anna held some affection for the man. James wasn't certain why he cared. He knew only that he did.

A rather unfortunate realization.

# CHAPTER SIX

Sipping her tea from a china cup, Annalisa stood at the railing on the quarterdeck, the wind billowing her skirt out behind her. To the east the sun was just coming over the horizon. She loved this time of morning, particularly today. Last night Sterling had stood at her desk and charted a route that would give them enough leagues to cover for today if the wind held true. He'd not plotted the entire course toward their destination, but he'd set them in the right direction.

"Drinking tea on the quarterdeck?" a deep voice asked.

Turning, she smiled slightly at Sterling. He looked less ragged. Having the freedom of the ship seemed to agree with him.

"It makes me feel civilized," she answered.

"I heard once that Black Bart sips tea on the deck of his ship."

"Black Bart is a ruthless pirate. I have nothing in common with him. I'm a privateer. There's a distinction."

"Subtle, to be sure. Some would argue none at all."

"I'm not doing anything dishonorable. I'm trying to recapture what was stolen from us."

Sterling leaned forward, his forearms resting on the rail, his hands clasped in front of him. His long hair was pulled back, held in place with a strip of leather. The wind toyed with his white lawn shirt, causing it to flutter slightly.

"Perhaps whether one is seen as a pirate or a privateer depends upon where the one looking is standing," he said. "You kidnapped me."

"You're not innocent. You have a bounty on your head. Any action taken against you is justified." She felt a spark of guilt. Not everything she was doing was sanctioned by the Crown.

"Does Black Bart sail these waters?" she asked, to change the subject.

"From time to time. His ship is *Royal Fortune*. His Jolly Roger is black. It has him and death holding an hourglass. If you should spy it, you'll want to head in the other direction."

"I think I'd rather face him."

"Trust me, m'lady, he's much worse than Crimson. He takes no prisoners."

"Have you ever fought him?"

"Nay, and I have no desire to. It's a sure path to death."

As was the path he was currently traveling, but she saw no point in reminding him of that.

"You're up early," she said to lighten the mood.

"Your quartermaster snores."

"You could always return to the brig."

"I think not. I'll adjust."

Taking another sip of tea, she studied him over the rim of her cup. "You don't speak in the manner I expected of a pirate. You speak almost like a gentleman who would fancy drinking tea in a garden in the afternoon."

Keeping one arm resting on the railing, he faced her. "That's Crimson's doing."

"The barbaric pirate? He taught you to speak like a gentleman?"

He shrugged, a corner of his mouth lifting.

"That's not an answer," she said. "Did he or didn't he?"

"What will you trade me for the tale?"

"Give it to me with no bartering."

"That's not the pirate way."

"Yes, well, right now you're serving aboard my ship, so you're not a pirate."

"I'm always a pirate, m'lady."

Her stomach dropped. Why did he have to be so constantly difficult? And why did she always find him extremely intriguing? Why did she like it when they parried words back and forth?

"I order you to tell me or spend a night in the brig."

He grinned. "You're a hard captain."

Her breath caught. Was he flirting with her? Was she flirting with him?

"Your tale?" she prodded.

"I suppose there's no harm in telling you. Crimson was educated at Oxford."

"A gentleman pirate?" She almost scoffed, but she didn't want to offend him. To her mortification, she enjoyed talking with him. "I don't believe you. I heard him calling out for you on the *Horizon*. He sounded uncouth."

"Playacting."

She waited but he said nothing else. She gave him a pointed look. "You're not going to leave it at that, are you? So he thinks the sea is his theater, a ship nothing more than a stage?"

"In a way I suppose he does. When we're at sea, he dresses like a gentleman." He dropped his gaze to her china cup. "He drinks tea. But when a ship is spotted on the horizon, he goes belowdecks and changes. When he reemerges, he's different. His clothes are the colorful garb of a pirate. His language is coarse. He talks as though he has no education at all."

"You do realize he's a madman?"

"Depends where you're standing." He held her gaze. "Are you aware that pirates are a democratic lot? We elect our captains. Who elected you, m'lady?"

"It's my ship, my quest. Therefore, I issue the orders." She angled her chin. "I daresay I can't say much for the intelligence of a crew who'd elect a man such as Crimson to oversee them."

"He's clever, he's brave —"

"He's brutal. Is it true he drinks the blood of his victims?" She couldn't believe she was asking.

"Crimson once told me that the reputation

for doing something can be as effective as doing it."

"Have you ever seen him do it?"

He slowly shook his head. "But don't tell a soul. Else he might decide he does have to do it."

"Do what?"

They both turned at the unexpected question. Nathaniel stood there, his blond hair long enough to curl playfully beneath his tricornered hat.

"We were just discussing Crimson Kelly and whether the rumors of his disgusting habits are true," Annalisa told him.

"I don't think Sterling should have free rein of the ship," he said sternly.

"I'm not interested in escape, mate. At least not yet."

"It's not your escape that concerns me but your ability to sabotage the ship." He looked at Anna, holding her gaze. "I don't trust him, Anna."

She nodded. "You're right, of course. Assign someone to watch him closely, but no shackles."

"Kane!" Nathaniel called over his shoulder.

The burly man stepped forward. "Aye, sir."

"Put Sterling to work swabbing the deck."

"Aye, sir. This way, mate."

Annalisa knew that Nathaniel had ordered the lowest form of duty for the pirate. It was an insult of the highest regard, something offered as punishment or because a man didn't possess the skills for anything else. So she wasn't surprised when Sterling objected.

"This wasn't part of our arrangement," he said.

"Every man on the ship pulls his weight or he goes in the brig," Nathaniel said.

"I provide the course."

"I'm not sure I trust it. You could take us in circles before we caught on."

"What would I gain?"

"I don't know."

"Nathaniel, we all agreed to this arrangement yesterday," she reminded him.

"I don't like it."

"Yes, well, that's the way it is. Is there something else you needed?"

"It's time for your morning practice."

"Oh, yes, of course. I'd forgotten. Laddie!"

A young boy stepped forward smartly, took her cup, and scurried away.

Annalisa drew out her cutlass. She suddenly

felt self-conscious with Sterling standing there, giving her a speculative look.

"You should go down below, Sterling, to avoid getting nicked," Nathaniel said as though reading her unease.

Annalisa wasn't surprised that Sterling simply crossed his arms over his chest and leaned against the railing. "I'd rather stay and watch."

"Nathaniel's right. The lessons can get quite vigorous."

"I'll take my chances."

"Very well."

She stepped forward to the middle of the deck and took her stance.

Nathaniel did the same. "Ready?"

She nodded.

When he swung his sword around, she deflected the blow, as always surprised by the force of the impact and the way her arm shook. They both pulled back. She struck. His sword met hers.

She jumped back. Circled slowly, watching him, watching his sword.

Then she became aware of the laughter. It started as a low rumble of amusement and grew louder. She turned to glare at Sterling.

"You find this amusing?" she asked.

"I do. You fight as though you're standing in a parlor."

"I'm still learning."

"The problem isn't you, m'lady. It's your tutor."

"I suppose you think you could do a better job," Nathaniel said.

"Have you any experience fighting pirates?" Sterling asked.

"Of course. I fought several when you attacked the *Horizon*."

"Ah, that explains your immense dislike of me." He stepped forward, held his hand out to Anna. "Give me your sword. I'll demonstrate what you can truly expect when you come up against pirates."

"You'll never carry a weapon on this ship, Sterling," Nathaniel said.

Sterling moved swiftly, snatching Anna's sword from her fingers before she knew what he was about. He arced it over his head and brought it down on Nathaniel—

Annalisa gasped in horror.

Dropping to a knee, Nathaniel raised his sword to deflect the blow. The clash of steel echoed over the deck.

"A pirate will never ask if you're ready," Sterling said.

Nathaniel shoved him, sending him back, but his balance hardly seemed affected. Nathaniel jumped to his feet.

Sterling struck again and again, but Nathaniel skillfully met each rapid-fire thrust and parry, backing up until he was pressed against the railing with nowhere to go.

"A pirate will attack quickly," Sterling said.

He leaped away, grabbed Annalisa, snaked his arm around her, holding her close against his chest, the fine edge of the sword hovering beneath her chin.

Her heart was pounding so loudly, she was certain all could hear it.

"A pirate will not fight fairly," Sterling said near her ear, his warm breath skimming over her cheek. "Do you really want to be taught how to fight pirates by a man with so little experience at defending himself against them?"

She lifted her foot and slammed it down on his toe. Yelping, he loosened his hold, and it was enough for her to slip beyond his reach. "Kane!" she yelled, holding out her hand, and the man who was supposed to be guarding

Sterling tossed her his cutlass. She caught it by the hilt, swung it around.

Sterling met her steel with his. The vibration nearly stunned her.

He struck, she struck back. They continued, dancing over the deck, their feet moving quickly, each blow coming faster than the next. All the while she was vaguely aware of Nathaniel calling for the men, the sound of rushing footsteps.

While she concentrated on each move, tried to anticipate where he'd strike, Sterling did little more than smile.

"That's right, m'lady —"

*Clash!*

"As fast and hard as you can —"

*Clang!*

"Attack. With no thought to wound, only to kill. The first blow makes a man your enemy."

*Clash!*

"The final blow must ensure he never comes after you."

*Clash! Clang! Clank! Clink!*

Over and over he swung his sword. Over and over she met each thrust.

Then she stumbled, found herself pressed against the mast, with the sword again at her throat.

"And never, ever let a pirate corner you," Sterling said in a low, dangerous voice.

"Step away from her, Sterling," Nathaniel ordered.

"It seems our lesson has come to an end," Sterling said.

She nodded, breathless from the exertion, from his nearness. "Until tomorrow, anyway."

Something danced in his eyes: a challenge, a bit of pleasure, some mischief. He was enjoying this much too much.

To her immense shame, so was she.

"Sterling —"

"It's all right, Nathaniel," Annalisa said.

She felt Sterling ease the pressure. With a nod, she stepped aside. The men descended on him like vultures, taking the sword and beating him to his knees, until his hands were bound behind his back and his head bent.

"I warned you," Nathaniel said. "He can't be trusted."

"If he couldn't be trusted, I'd be dead. Unhand him now," she ordered.

Sterling lifted his head, his gaze homing in on her as though he couldn't quite believe the command.

"It was merely a lesson," she said.

"Anna —" Nathaniel began.

"He was right, Nathaniel. You've taught me a good deal about swordplay, but your heart has never been in it. I'm certain that's because you expect me to hide belowdecks when the time comes. But I shan't. I'll stand and fight this time. I need someone with experience at fighting ruthlessly to teach me. Perhaps we all do."

She glanced at Sterling who was standing, no longer bound. "A little warning next time that it's practice."

"As I said, a pirate will give you no warning."

She nodded. "Go see the doctor. Have him check your back, make sure all this activity didn't reopen the wounds. Mr. Kane will escort you."

While the deck cleared of onlookers, Annalisa walked back to the railing. Her heart was only now beginning to slow.

Nathaniel stepped nearer. "I don't like the attention you give him. You must know that you and you alone are the reason I'm aboard this ship."

She had known. And she'd used it. She'd used every means at her disposal to get the ship and crew. She'd offered them a meager portion of the gold as a reward — when they reacquired it. The men followed Nathaniel because he earned their respect. He followed her because he cared for her. As a young officer aboard the *Horizon* when she'd traveled on it with her father, he'd shown a shy interest in her.

"Surely you want some sort of retribution," she said.

His jaw tightened. "I can't deny I want to see Crimson Kelly hanged. But I want to see it of Sterling, too."

"I promised him his freedom."

"And we'll grant it to him. But a tiger can't change its stripes. He'll return to pirating. And eventually he'll be hanged."

That thought saddened her more than she thought possible.

"Can we please talk of something else?"

He nodded. The silence eased around them. It seemed they had nothing else to talk about.

*　　*　　*

Ferret made his way through the narrow passageway. Having lost an arm worked to his advantage sometimes. He could squeeze into tight places where many a man couldn't. Might come in handy during battle.

Turning the corner, he found himself pressed up against the wall, a large hand wrapped around his throat. He was dancing on his toes, squeaking.

"Shut up, Ferret," James Sterling said.

"Can't breathe," he rasped.

"Pity."

But he heard no pity in Sterling's voice.

"I didn't betray ye." He gasped. His vision was turning black at the edges. "Just saw a chance . . . to make a bit of coin."

"By turning me in."

"Then helping ye escape. It's why I'm here."

Suddenly released, he crumpled to the floor. He pressed his hand to his throat. His windpipe didn't feel crushed. Cautiously, he glanced up at Sterling who had crossed his arms over his chest and was staring down on him.

Quickly, he crouched. Ferret screeched and

pressed his back against the wall, wishing he could disappear.

"I knew you'd turn me in for the reward," Sterling said quietly. "I was surprised it took you so long."

"If ye knew then, why . . ."

"Because I wanted to be caught." He touched his finger to his temple. "You're a small man, Ferret. You think of immediate rewards, and those tend to be insignificant. I concentrate on larger gains, and while they often take more time to acquire, they tend to be more valuable."

"I don't know what ye be talkin' about."

"I know. But now it is you who owes me."

"I'll give ye half the reward."

"Keep it all. It's a mere pittance compared with what I want."

"What do ye want?"

"Your help when the time comes."

"And when will that be?"

James Sterling did little more than smile.

# CHAPTER SEVEN

It was the sort of laughter that James had never before heard. He'd heard robust laughter. Boisterous laughter. Bawdy laughter.

But joyous laughter?

He had no recollection of hearing anything as sweet as the sound that now bubbled up from Anna's throat. Her soft trilling floated over the ship. It added harmony to the lively strains of the fiddle that a crewman was playing.

They were celebrating the day of her birth — today. The cook had made a pudding, and everyone had taken a spoonful. As the sun had begun to set, the wind calmed, and now the ship was barely slicing through the water.

Most of the men were on the deck. A few brave souls ventured forth to dance a jig with Anna. It was the reason for her laughter. With her skirts raised above her ankles, she was dancing as merrily as the man with whom she was now partnered. He was exaggerating his steps, acting the fool, making her laugh all the harder.

Not that James blamed him. He thought he might do almost anything to be the one responsible for releasing that intoxicating sound.

But he had yet to determine how to make her laugh, like that at least. When she was with him, she was all seriousness. For more than a week now, he'd been teaching her close-quarters fighting. He'd taught her how to use the cutlass to draw a man in near enough that she could jab him with her dagger.

James had a couple of nicks to serve as proof that she was learning quickly and learning well. She did like to play dirty.

Her eagerness astounded him, as did her ability for the unexpected. She was small, and more than once he'd underestimated her. She'd trip him. Or move out of the way so quickly that if not for the fact that he was accustomed to moving with the roiling of the ship, he might have tumbled.

And of course, as always, Northrup was there, watching like a hawk. As though the man thought James was fool enough to try a blatant escape. No, when his escape came, it would be when he had nothing to lose and a great deal to gain.

He noticed Northrup talking with the man playing the fiddle. Suddenly, the tempo of the music shifted into something slower, softer. Anna stopped dancing. James could see her chest rising and falling as she fought for air after her exertions.

Northrup moved nearer to her and held out his hand. An invitation. An ownership. James wasn't certain which, but he didn't like it. Didn't fancy the way her eyes sparkled. The way the crew moved back to give them more room. Or the manner in which she placed her hand in Northrup's.

And then they were dancing. Something slow. He held her hand up and they circled. Then they switched hands and circled the other way, all the while holding each other's gaze as though nothing was quite as mesmerizing. As though no one else was aboard the ship.

James was caught off guard by the spark of jealousy that flared. And the bitterness that followed because he didn't have the knowledge required to dance with her. He didn't have the skills, he didn't have the education to fit into polite society.

At moments like this, it became ever more clear exactly what he was. A pirate.

It was his destiny.

"Looks like ye be wishin' to be dancin' with 'er," a raspy voice whispered.

Ferret. Since their talk belowdecks, he and James had met on several occasions, but all their meetings were held in secret. Escaping Kane's ever-watchful guard sometimes made it difficult.

"Why don't you run along and shriek like a cornered mouse someplace else?" James asked.

"I 'ad to be convincin'. Make 'er think I wanted nuthin' to do with ye."

"You overdid it a bit, matey."

Although, in truth, he didn't believe Ferret's claim that his plan all along had been to help James escape. But he saw no reason to reveal his thoughts on the matter. All that was important was that Ferret now do what was required of him.

"Better safe than sorry, I always say. And I'm payin' fer it. 'Er quartermaster has taken to callin' me 'Weasel.' The blighter."

"Weasel, ferret. What's the difference?"

"One is me name and one ain't."

James couldn't stop himself from smiling. Ferret got indignant over the silliest of things.

"Considerin' what they did to yer back and the way Northrup keeps 'is eye on ye, I ain't so sure yer plan's workin'."

"Have no fear. It's working. You'd best be off, now. Wouldn't do for us to be seen together."

"Aye, Cap'n."

James reached out and grabbed Ferret's arm before he could get away. "Watch your words. You'll jinx me. I'm not captain yet."

Ferret's mouth spread into a calculating grin. "But ye will be."

James released him and looked back at the celebrating men.

"Aye," he said quietly. "I will be."

*　　*　　*

Lying in her bunk, Annalisa couldn't sleep. She should have been worn out from all the dancing. Instead, she longed for an open field to run through. She wanted to gather flowers and leap over bushes.

There had been something in Nathaniel's eyes when they'd danced. A spark. Warm, inviting. Something that said this journey wouldn't be the only one they'd make together.

She couldn't deny that he was handsome. And strong. And courageous. And noble.

Everything that James Sterling wasn't.

So why had she found herself wishing that the pirate would cross the deck and dance with her? She'd seen him standing off to the side, not part of the activities. She couldn't deny that she'd felt a pang of pity for him. He didn't belong here. And that fact had her feeling pity for herself.

Clambering out of bed, she quickly donned a simple dress. Then she grabbed the lantern from her desk and went out into the hallway. The only sounds were the creaking of the ship.

It was late and the men were sleeping. Other than the early morning when the ship was just coming awake, this was her favorite time. After it had gone to sleep.

She understood why men referred to ships as ladies. Why they gave them names. Why they cared for them. It was almost as though the ship was a living, breathing thing. She was surprised by how much she was coming to love this life on the sea.

As she walked to the door leading to the quarterdeck, she couldn't deny that a part of her regretted that she'd promised to give Nathaniel this ship as his reward for helping her. On deck, she acknowledged the man standing watch at the helm. She glanced up at the crow's nest. She couldn't see the man on watch, but she knew he was there.

She made her way to the prow of the ship and set down the lantern. Placing her arms on the railing, she leaned forward and breathed in the salt air. She heard what sounded like a distant horn.

"What *is* that?" she wondered aloud.

"A whale."

She spun around, her heart hammering. James Sterling stood there, muscled arms crossed over his broad chest. After a week of practicing swordplay, she'd become very familiar with exactly how strong and skilled he was. She was still nagged by how easy taking him had been. If he'd put up a rousing resistance, she had little doubt their physician would have been kept busy all night taking care of all the wounds Sterling would have inflicted.

"Why aren't you asleep?" she asked, irritated with him for being here, irritated with herself because she was glad of his presence.

"Northrup snores."

"So you've said before."

"Why aren't you asleep?"

"I simply couldn't sleep." An increasingly frequent occurrence, as he haunted her dreams. She turned her attention to the inky black sea. "The sky is so vast out here. It makes me feel so . . . insignificant."

"You could never be insignificant."

There was something in his voice. An undercurrent that was decidedly dangerous. She was grateful for an opportunity to change the subject. She pointed toward the sky. "Look, there's a star falling. Where does it go? Do you think it falls into the ocean?"

"Of course. I've seen them there. They come to life once they hit the water."

Laughing lightly, she glanced over at him. "I don't believe you."

"I can show you if you like."

"You can show me living stars?"

"At Crimson's island. The water is so clear that when you walk out in it, you can see your feet . . . and all the creatures that live there. Among them are the stars."

"I doubt we'll have time to go scavenging." But she was intrigued by the notion. "How much longer until we get there?"

"We get there when we get there."

"Nathaniel is beginning to doubt that you know where the island is. He thinks you're toying with us."

"I don't really care what Northrup thinks. What do you think?"

"That you have nothing to gain by delaying our arrival."

He smiled broadly in the moonlight. "Exactly. Why would I put off gaining my freedom?"

"I'm not sure. Where's your guard?" she asked.

"Sleeping. He snores, as well."

"We'll have to assign another one then."

"If it makes you feel safer."

She wasn't certain anything would make her feel safer until he was off her ship.

"I saw you dancing earlier," he said.

"Why didn't you join in?"

"Was I invited?"

"I suppose not."

The words felt cruel, but they were honest. If he had approached her, she wasn't at all certain she'd have danced with him. It would have been uncomfortable with the others watching. And what would they have thought if she'd smiled at him as she had at Nathaniel? If she'd given any indication that she was enjoying herself?

He took a step nearer. "We could dance now."

She released a slight laugh. "There's no music now."

"Of course there is. How can you be deaf to it?"

She strained to listen. Were the men playing belowdecks? She shook her head. "I don't hear it."

"How can you not hear the wind as it dances over the water?"

121

"We were talking of music."

"It is music. To me at least."

He was suddenly so very, very close.

"Listen to it. Close your eyes and listen," he urged.

She was incredibly tempted, but not with him this near. "I can listen just as well with my eyes open."

"Hear the water, the wind, and that whale. It's all music."

Turning, she faced away from him, faced the sea. "It's a lonely sound."

She was acutely aware of him coming up behind her, putting his arms on either side of her, and grabbing the railing. Perhaps she'd even invited his nearness.

"Not so lonely," he whispered near her ear.

For the longest time, they stood there with neither of them moving, listening to the sea.

"Anna," he rasped.

It was the first time he'd ever called her by name. In his voice, she heard the longing that mirrored her own. She was vaguely aware that she'd turned, that his arms were suddenly holding her close, that she was looking up into his eyes . . .

He dipped his head and kissed her.

And it was as though the tempest had returned. A storm of desire swept through her. While she knew it was wrong to want to kiss him, she lacked the will to withdraw.

Everything about this moment was wrong. And yet she couldn't deny that she never wanted it to end. With his lips against hers, she could hear the music of the sea. Or perhaps it was only her heart singing. She'd never known anything as wondrous.

He drew back, a cocky grin on his face. "That one I didn't steal. That one you gave willingly. I wonder how your Mr. Northrup will feel about that when he finds out."

The sound of her palm hitting his cheek resounded around them. "You're no gentleman, sir."

"That's exactly why you're drawn to me. I think you like that I'm a pirate. I bring adventure to your safe little world."

"You destroyed my safe little world," she spat. "I despise you and all you stand for."

"Keep telling yourself that, m'lady. Maybe you'll come to believe it."

She wanted to slap him again. Instead, she

turned on her heel and headed back to her quarters, leaving him standing there. His words struck a little too close to the truth.

James watched as Anna trudged back to her cabin. It was all he could do not to go after her. He'd spoken his words knowing they'd make her angry enough to walk away. And he needed her to walk away because he wanted her to stay so badly.

The kiss had unsettled him. Before, she'd been at his mercy. This time, he'd been at hers.

She'd looked so beautiful standing there, gazing out to sea. Crimson had once told him a tale about Sirens, magical creatures that lived on an island. Their songs lured mariners to their destruction — their ships were destroyed by the rocks surrounding the island. And even knowing that death awaited them, they couldn't resist the lure of the Sirens' song.

James had felt that way. That he was being lured to his destruction. He was a pirate. It was in his blood.

Anna was a lady who would one day return

to sipping tea in her parlor instead of on the deck of a ship.

Harboring any true feelings for her would be disastrous to his plans for obtaining a ship and returning to his pirating ways.

He had to keep her at bay. Even if it meant hurting her.

If faced with choosing between his destruction or hers . . . he'd always choose hers.

# CHAPTER EIGHT

"Are you truly a pirate, sir?"

James had been standing on the quarterdeck waiting for Anna to appear for their morning lesson, wondering if perhaps after their encounter last night she'd not show. He'd hardly blame her if she didn't. It would be best for both of them.

He glanced down at the young lad who'd spoken. "And who might you be?" he asked.

"Sam. Samuel Baker. I'm a powder monkey."

"Are you now?"

"Aye. Mr. Northrup says I'm the best."

The best at carrying small buckets of powder to the cannon.

"I've never met a pirate before," the lad said.

"Well, Sam Baker, now you have."

"Did you really serve under Crimson Kelly?"

"Aye."

"Is it true what they say? Does he drink blood?"

He heard a gasp, and it was then that he noticed a few of the other lads gathered on the steps, peering up cautiously. He wondered how they'd come to be on this ship. If, like him, they were simply one mouth too many to feed.

"Aye, 'tis true," James said.

He watched as the boy grew pale. "So if we lose to him, he'll drink our blood?"

"Will he kill us first?" another lad asked, his eyes so large James was surprised they didn't pop out of his head.

James crouched down. "So ye be afraid?" he asked, making his voice less cultured.

The boys all looked at one another. James knew they were trying to determine who would be the first to acknowledge the fear. Once one did, they all would. He held up his left hand. "Do you see this ring?"

The boys nodded.

"A witch gave it to me. She put a spell on it.

You have but to spit on it, and Crimson Kelly will never take your blood."

"Truly?" Sam Baker asked.

"Ye 'ave me word."

"How does it stop him?" a smaller lad asked.

How indeed? James hadn't thought that far. He'd forgotten how inquisitive he'd been as a lad. Crimson had taken to allowing him to ask only three questions per day. Any more than that and he had to go without supper. He went to bed hungry many a night.

"Because when he looks at you, he sees his own death. And he knows your blood is poison to him."

Grinning, the lads all looked at one another, until finally Sam Baker asked, "May we spit on it, sir?"

"By all means."

He held out his hand and the boys filed past, each taking a turn at spitting on the ring.

When they were finished, Sam Baker asked, "How did you get your scar, sir?"

"Now, that, lad, is a tale best told on a moonless night."

"Will you come down to the crew's quarters and tell us some night?"

James wouldn't be here that long, and lies were easier to spill than the truth. "Aye, lad, I will."

"Don't you lads have duties?" Anna asked from behind James.

He grimaced and wondered how long she'd been there. While the boys scurried away, James slowly unfolded his body and wiped his hand on his shirt.

When he turned around, Anna was smiling. Not exactly the reaction he'd expected of her this morning. He'd expected her to be wielding the cat-o'-nine.

"A witch gave you the ring?" she asked, her eyebrow arched.

"A very lovely witch." He grimaced. It was so much easier to flirt with her than to anger her. More pleasant as well. "'Tis cursed, however."

"Indeed."

"It's the reason Crimson marooned me. Because I took the ring instead of the girl. I shan't make that mistake again."

"Do you spit on the ring?"

"Every morning."

She laughed, that wonderful, joyous laugh she had. That Siren song that was so dangerous to him.

"I hadn't expected you to talk to me this morning," he admitted.

"Honestly, I hadn't planned to, but then I saw you with the young lads . . ."

She gnawed on the lower lip that he was so tempted to lean over and kiss.

"You were so kind to them," she finally continued.

"I lied to them."

Sadness settled in her eyes. "So Crimson will kill them and take their blood?"

"No, he'll take them and turn them into pirates."

"Not if I have my way. We'll capture him and put an end to his tyranny of the high seas." She raised her cutlass. "And to that end, I need a lesson."

He tilted his head. "Aye, aye, Captain."


With the wind whipping through her hair, Annalisa stood at the prow. She'd finished her lesson a short time ago. Her arm was sore from the continual onslaught of blows. But she also had to admit that it thrilled her that Sterling was testing her mettle as thoroughly as he was.

She was confident that when the time came, she'd be up to the task of fighting a pirate.

"Look," Sterling said, beside her and pointing just off the prow.

Playful gray dolphins were swimming in front of the ship.

Smiling brightly, Annalisa leaned forward. "It's almost as though they're racing us."

"It does appear that way."

"They seem so friendly."

"They are. I've swum with them."

Annalisa stiffened, aware of the fact that beside her, Sterling did the same. Very slowly, she turned to face him. "I thought you said you couldn't swim."

He scratched the end of his nose, furrowed his brow. "Did I?"

"You did. So now the question before me is which is the lie: Can you not swim at all, or did you swim with dolphins?"

"Let me know when you figure it out."

When she not only figured that out, but also how many other lies he might have told her.

"Do you know where Crimson Kelly's island is?" she asked.

"I do."

"If you're lying, I'll hang you myself."

He gave her a devilish grin. "I want him as much as you do, Anna. He marooned me. For most men that's a death sentence."

"Then he no doubt thinks you're dead now."

"No doubt. Which gives us an advantage. He won't be expecting us at the island."

"Does it have a name?"

"He calls it Devil's Gate."

A shiver went through her. "I suppose he sees it as the way into hell."

"Or perhaps as the way out. After all, that's where he hoards all his misbegotten gains. Perhaps he thinks he'll buy his way into heaven."

She bit her lower lip. "You lied about not being able to swim."

"What gave me away?"

"The timing of the lies. When you lied about swimming, you didn't trust us and we didn't trust you. Now you have no reason to lie."

"Perhaps I lied about the dolphins to impress you."

Her heart hammered against her chest. "Why would you feel a need to impress me?"

"For the same reason that every man aboard this ship does. You're very lovely."

"Are you saying that every man aboard this ship lies?"

"I suspect more so than you realize."

She couldn't imagine Nathaniel telling an untruth or in any way deceiving her. Sterling was no doubt viewing the world from his perspective of piracy.

"How did you come to be a pirate?"

"I was aboard a pirate ship."

She rolled her eyes at him. "How did you come to be aboard a pirate ship?"

He tightened his jaw, and she didn't think he'd tell her.

"My mother had too many mouths to feed," he finally said.

"She gave you to the pirates?" she asked, horrified by the notion.

He shrugged. "Where do you think your little powder monkeys come from?"

"I thought they were orphans."

"No doubt."

"Or young men wanting a better life."

"Perhaps."

"You're rather cynical."

"I am indeed."

She looked back down at the water. The dolphins were still swimming ahead of them. She wondered if they ever grew tired. She turned back to Sterling. "On a moonless night when you tell the lads how you came to have your scar, I'd like to be there to hear the tale."

"There's really not much to it. My first battle. I didn't duck quickly enough."

"And for that you need a moonless night?"

"Makes for a better story in the dark."

"I suppose you'll embellish it for the lads."

"Of course."

"Don't frighten them."

"Do you truly think a man who would allow them to spit on his hand would find sport in terrifying children?"

"Quite honestly, James Sterling, I don't know what to think of you." She took a step away from him. "If you'll excuse me, I need to see to business."

She began walking across the deck with a speed that rivaled that of the dolphins in the water. She caught sight of Nathaniel standing on the poop deck watching her. There was obvious disapproval in his stance.

She knew she shouldn't enjoy spending time with a pirate.

Unfortunately, however, she did.


"I'm telling you. He's leading us on a merry goose chase. Up and down the Caribbean. Making fools of us," Nathaniel said.

Anna stood behind the helmsman. She didn't understand the particulars of how maneuvering the ship worked, but she still found it fascinating to watch, even when they were doing nothing more than traveling in a straight line.

"Anna, it's been ten days," Nathaniel added, the exasperation clear in his voice.

"I know."

"How long do you intend to let this go on?"

"Until we arrive at the island."

"And how long before you accept that we're not going to be arriving at any island? You've given him his freedom to roam about the ship. You've removed his incentive."

"What would you have me do?"

"Put him back in the brig. Make his life miserable. Give him a reason to uphold his end of the bargain as quickly as possible."

"Putting him in the brig will not speed things along. We just have to be patient."

Nathaniel took her hand. "It is becoming more difficult for me to do that. If I may be so bold, once this adventure is behind us, I'm hoping —"

"Land ho! Land ho!"

Annalisa jerked her head up to see the crow's nest. The lookout was pointing east. She pulled her spyglass open and peered through it. She could see the green, mountainous island in the distance.

"Do you suppose that's it?" she asked, her heart hammering.

"I doubt it. Has it occurred to you that he could be leading us into a trap?"

"A trap would require assistance."

"Perhaps, but I think we should trim back the sails and approach slowly and cautiously."

She nodded. "Where's Sterling?" Before anyone could respond, she yelled, "Sterling! James Sterling!"

Then she saw him, standing at the prow of the ship.

"Come along," she ordered Nathaniel.

She hurried across the ship, wending her

way around the men who'd stopped working, hoping to catch a glimpse of the island in the distance. When she finally reached Sterling, she was breathless.

"Is that it?" she asked, holding out her spyglass.

He took it from her, peered through it. "Aye."

"I see no signs of the *Phantom Mist*," Nathaniel said.

"It could be on the other side of the island," Annalisa said, unable to keep the anticipation from her voice. They were so close to seeing the completion of their quest.

"Let's hope not," Sterling said.

She jerked her head around to look at him. "Why not?"

"Let's go to your cabin, and I'll explain."

Using the backside of one of Anna's maps, James drew a squiggly outline of the island.

"On the far side is a narrow, shallow cove. It runs inland for a good distance. Your ship is shallow bottomed enough that it can easily travel into the cove. It'll be hidden there. You'll set up lookouts at the entrance of the cove. When they spot Crimson returning, we'll be in a position to surprise him and take him."

"We could be waiting there for months," Northrup stated, his arms crossed over his chest.

"It's possible. Have something else more important to do with your time, matey?" James asked.

"If I'd known this was your plan, I'd have never agreed to it. Crimson is supposed to be here."

"And will be."

"But we have no way of knowing when." Northrup turned to Anna. "We should stay on the sea and search for him."

"And just where are you going to search?" James asked, feeling an irrational need to have her follow his advice and not Northup's. He felt as though he was engaged in battle. An insane notion. "He could be anywhere. The one thing we are assured of is that he always returns here after a raid, to bury his treasure."

"But we have no way of knowing when he'll raid a ship or when he'll have treasure to bury."

"He'll arrive during the dark of the moon."

Anna straightened and stared at him. "How do you know?"

"He's a man of habit. He always comes to the island during the dark of the moon."

"That should be within the week then."

"Aye."

She nodded. "Then we'll wait for him."

"I don't like the notion of going into a cove where we could be trapped," Northrup said.

"Are there any of my ideas you favor?" James asked.

"None that I can think of."

"We captured him specifically for this purpose, Nathaniel," Anna said, her voice laced with exasperation.

"I want more men on guard at night," Northrup said.

"You shall have it."

"And I want two guards on Sterling at all times."

James watched Annalisa's face, saw her struggling with a decision. Against her better judgment she'd come to trust him.

"Not a problem, mate," James said. "Make it three. Four. A dozen. Believe it or not, I want to see Crimson Kelly securely imprisoned aboard this ship as much as you do."

"Oh, I doubt that," Northrup said.

James didn't bother to argue, because the truth was, he doubted anyone — not even Anna — wanted to see Crimson Kelly captured more than he did.

# CHAPTER NINE

"It's a little like paradise here," Annalisa said. She stood calf deep in the warm waters of the cove.

They'd sailed easily into it late the afternoon before. Last night, there'd been no moon. Anna had barely slept with the realization that her quest might soon come to a satisfactory end. She'd assigned men in shifts of four to watch the area from the mouth of the cove so they'd know when Crimson Kelly arrived.

This morning, Sterling had knocked on her door with the sun and enticed her into joining him for some exploring. She could certainly understand why Crimson Kelly liked the island. It was so incredibly green, the water so marvelously blue from a distance, but clear as glass up close. And so inviting.

Without hesitation, she'd brought the back of her skirt forward, between her legs, and tucked it into her belt. The action had raised the front and sides almost to her knees. She'd created baggy breeches. She'd removed her shoes and stockings and now walked along the water's edge within the cove. Around her ankles colorful fish and sea creatures darted here and there. They came in close for inspection, then darted away. The water was so clear and pure here that she could see her wiggling toes.

"I've always liked it," James said.

"Does Crimson spend a lot of time here?"

"More and more of late. He's seen nearly thirty years. That's old for a pirate."

"And what about you? How many years have you seen?"

"One and twenty."

"You seem older."

He grinned his cocky grin. "The result of hard living and even harder playing."

She couldn't help herself. She laughed joyously. James Sterling could be such fun.

Playful and teasing. "At moments like this, I could almost forget you're a pirate."

At moments like this, James almost wished he wasn't. When she looked at him like that, with such openness, he was almost ashamed of his past . . . and his future.

He'd rolled up the legs on his breeches so he could walk in the water beside her. He'd rolled up the arms on his shirt, so he could —

"Here," he said, scooping his hand through the water to lift out his find. "I told you the stars that fall from the sky land here."

He didn't think she could have given him a brighter smile if he'd dug up a treasure chest for her.

Tentatively, she moved her hand toward his, then flinched as though surprised. "It moved!"

"Of course."

"It's alive. Who would have thought?" She lifted her gaze, full of wonder and awe, to his. "Who would have thought a pirate would notice such things as the creatures that live in the sea?"

He tossed the starfish back into the water so it could go scrounging for food. He was a bit uncomfortable that he'd shared his find with her. He'd barely slept last night, knowing their time together would soon end. He'd had an insane need to share the island with her, to pretend for a short spell that they were like normal people, instead of what they were: a pirate in search of wealth and a pirate hunter in search of justice.

James knew he was more likely to acquire his goal than she was hers.

"I noticed a lot of things about the island," he felt compelled to explain. He leaned toward her slightly and smiled wickedly. "We spent a lot of time here, and I was always searching for Crimson's buried treasure."

"Are you sure it's buried around here somewhere?"

"Absolutely. If the chest was light, Crimson carried it himself to wherever he was taking it. If it was heavy, he blindfolded the men who carried it, tied a rope about their waists, and led them like mules."

"Then why blind them and leave them to roam the island afterward?"

"An additional precaution."

He watched as she shuddered. He didn't

know why he was telling her these elaborate tales.

"I thought I could hear the mournful wail of the lost souls last night," she said.

"It was just the wind blowing through the cove."

"But what if it's not? What if it really is all the men he left here to die?"

James looked around. He'd never been fearful of this place, but he couldn't deny that there was an eeriness to it. "Then mayhaps they'll help us capture him."

"He's an awful man, isn't he?"

"Legend would have you think so."

Her eyes widened slightly. "You don't think so?"

He shrugged. "He started out as a privateer during Queen Anne's War. At her command, he raided French and Spanish ships. But it's hard to give up what you've risked life and limb to obtain. And when the Crown suddenly has no use for you, what else is a man to do?"

"Are you justifying his piracy?"

"No, but I understand it. What are you going to do, Anna, if when you find the treasure you seek, you also find others?"

He could see her pondering the ramifications of his question.

"None of it comes with a note saying to whom it belongs, you know," he prodded.

Part of him hoped she'd take the bait, consider the life of a pirate, and part of him hoped she'd stand by the convictions she held that he could never embrace.

She reached down, scooped up some water, and flicked it at him. "You're ruining a perfectly wonderful morning."

He laughed. "You're tempted to keep it."

She stuck her nose in the air. "Not at all."

Reaching out, he grabbed her and pulled her close. "I think there's a bit of pirate in you, Anna."

Looking into his eyes that were as green as the sea, Annalisa almost admitted that perhaps there was. She'd come to love the feel of the ship beneath her, but even more, she'd come to love the absence of restrictions. She could come and go as she pleased. She was captain of her own ship, in charge of her own destiny. And who was there to object if she found herself falling in love with a pirate?

Only her own heart knew her time in this world was temporary.

She wondered if Sterling knew what she was thinking, the paths down which her thoughts traveled. His eyes seemed to reflect the realization of dreams that would never be held.

His fingers, so warm, skimmed along her cheek. "Anna," he whispered, and lowered his mouth to hers.

It was wrong, so wrong, to want him to kiss her. It was wicked, so wicked, to enjoy it as much as she did. She wanted this moment to go on forever. Here in this paradise.

"Cap'n! Cap'n!"

Annalisa broke away and looked in the direction of the shouts. Sam Baker was racing toward her, an urgency in his movements.

"Cap'n, we spotted a ship on the horizon. We think it's the *Phantom Mist!*"

At the edge of the bluff, hidden behind shrubbery, Annalisa held the spyglass to her eye. It was a galleon. And while she couldn't make out its name, she could see the very distinctive figurehead — a ferocious pouncing lion, its mouth wide as though it intended to gobble up its prey.

"That's him, isn't it?" Annalisa asked, holding the spyglass out to James who was crouched beside her.

He took the spyglass and peered through it. "Aye, that's him."

"How long before he gets here?"

"Judging by the billow in his sails, he should be here by nightfall."

"Then we've no time to lose," Nathaniel said. He was crouched on the other side of Annalisa. "We need to prepare to meet him head-on."

"That's a sure way to be defeated," James said.

"And what would you suggest?" Nathaniel asked.

Annalisa heard the sarcasm in his voice. She knew he wasn't truly interested in any suggestions Sterling might offer. Nathaniel still didn't trust him.

Sterling leaned back lazily against the boulder. "We wait."

"Until he arrives, traps us in the cove, and destroys us with a few well-aimed cannonballs? That's a jolly brilliant plan," Nathaniel snapped.

"We can see him, he can't see us. And he's

**148**

not going to head into the cove because he's not shallow bottomed. He'll drop anchor a ways out. He'll use longboats to get to shore, but not at night. He's superstitious in that way. Quite honestly, he thinks the island's haunted by all the men he's killed here. He only makes shore in the light of day."

He said no more, as though he'd given them all the information they needed. When Nathaniel held his tongue, Anna assumed that he was as confused as she. But since she trusted James more than Nathaniel did, she was comfortable asking, "Then how do you suggest we handle this situation?"

"Under cover of darkness, we go out in longboats. Board the ship. Take the prize."

"You make it sound so simple."

"Crimson attacks during the day, with cannons blasting and swords drawn, because he wants to strike terror into the hearts of all honest men who roam the seas. Terrorized men tend to surrender, and if you can terrorize them before ever spying them, so much the better. But we want the captain and his ship, both unharmed. Stealth will give us the advantage."

Annalisa looked at Nathaniel, silently asking his opinion.

"I don't like leaving the ship in the cove," he grumbled. "Feels too much like being a sitting duck."

"We won't remain in the cove for long," Annalisa assured him. "As soon as we've secured the *Phantom Mist*, we'll bring our ship into open waters. We'll need her brig, and we'll moor the *Phantom Mist* to her. And you'll need to choose a crew to sail her back to New Providence."

"I'll take that honor myself." Smiling almost sadly, he reached out and touched her cheek. "I think you're fully capable of sailing *The Dangerous Lady* without me."

She glanced over at Sterling. "Give us some privacy, please."

With nothing more than a nod, he clambered down to the shore.

She turned back to Nathaniel. "Nathaniel —"

"You've fallen in love with him, haven't you?" he said before she could say more.

She felt the tears burn her eyes. "I don't know."

"I think you do know. I think you just don't want to admit it because deep down you know you can't trust him. He's charmed you into forgetting that he's a scoundrel."

To her mortification, she feared that she was drawn to him *because* he was a scoundrel.

"He'll break your heart, Anna. And when he does, maybe you'll finally see that I'm the better man."

Before she could answer, he was scrambling down the slope.

She knew Nathaniel was the better choice. She knew he was undoubtedly the right choice.

Unfortunately for him — and her — it seemed her heart disagreed.

# CHAPTER TEN

Annalisa could hardly fathom the anticipation she was experiencing. All she'd worked to obtain, all she'd sacrificed for . . . it was finally within easy reach.

She'd just tucked her white shirt into her breeches when a knock sounded on her door. Her heart jolted. Was it time already?

She hurried to the door and swung it open. Lord help her. She didn't think Sterling had ever looked more dangerous. His dark shirt was tucked into his tight breeches. Those he'd tucked into his boots. A red scarf was tied around his arm, to signal he was one of them. She had one as well. All the crewmen who would be participating in tonight's exploits did. A black belt slung over his shoulder and across his back held three pistols. A sword hung at his hip. At least one knife was visible. She suspected he had at least one hidden somewhere on his person.

Nathaniel had argued vehemently against allowing James to have weapons. But he was the man who knew the plan, and to send him forth weaponless would be sending him to his death.

"You shouldn't wear white," James told her now. "It'll make you more visible in the darkness."

"I hadn't thought of that."

He gave her one of his devilish grins. "You probably didn't think of this, either."

He held out a bowl to her.

"Looks like mud," she said.

"It is. You need to put it on your face."

"No wonder pirates are always so dirty-looking." She took the bowl from him. "You're looking forward to this, aren't you?"

"Aren't you?"

Gnawing on her lip, she nodded quickly and dared to speak honestly. Something she could do with him without fear of judgment. Something she couldn't always do with Nathaniel. "And not for all the reasons that I should. It's awful, but I actually think it's going to be fun."

"Not fun so much as exciting. Pitting your swordsmanship against another's. Not knowing if the next beat of your heart will be your last."

She hadn't considered that. Hadn't truly considered that tonight men might die.

Reaching out, he trailed his finger along her cheek. "Don't worry, Anna. We're sneaking up on them. If all goes well, there'll be very little fighting." He kissed her hard and quick. "Just stay close to me and you'll be safe."

*Just stay close to me?*

What madness had possessed him to tell her that?

James sat in the longboat with her now, one of a dozen men rowing toward the *Phantom Mist*. It had dropped anchor exactly as James had known it would. Crimson was set in his ways. Lights were out at eight. No candles burning after that time. Right about now, he should be finishing off his evening grog. He'd stumble into bed and take to snoring louder than Nathaniel Northrup.

James's plan involved getting to Crimson first, before the man could begin shouting orders. James hadn't anticipated having Anna at his side when he met up with his former captain. He had a score to settle with him. And settle it he would, one way or another.

The four boats sliced silently through the water. No one spoke. They moved their oars in a nice steady rhythm that created nary a wake and nary a sound. There would be a man in the crow's nest, but he'd be looking out to sea, not on the deck of the ship. Unless he was sleeping, in which case he wouldn't be looking at all.

Nathaniel Northrup was going to see to him.

There would be a man standing watch at the helm. James would silence him. Then into the captain's cabin he'd slip.

With the girl at his side.

Devil take it! As much as he didn't want her there, he was equally glad that he'd be able to watch over her. He had experience fighting pirates. These blokes had very little. Anna was safer with him.

It was a strange thing to be worried over her welfare. He wasn't used to caring about anyone save himself. What did he care if she got hurt? His ultimate goal was possession of the ship.

There was a possibility she'd interfere with his plans.

He'd just have to see that she didn't.


Annalisa couldn't believe how quiet it all was. It seemed like when you were going into battle, there should be an abundance of noise. There should be drums, shouting, cannon fire.

But all she heard were the oars slicing through the water, drawing them nearer to the ship, and the maddeningly rapid pounding of her heart. She was surprised the erratic thrumming didn't alert the crew of the *Phantom Mist*.

Yet even with the blood rushing through her, she wasn't really afraid. She would be beside Sterling. And as improbable as it seemed, she trusted him to keep her safe more than any other man on her ship. Even Nathaniel.

She suspected Nathaniel would be disappointed to know that. But how could she explain what she felt for Sterling? It had sneaked up on her, just as they were sneaking up on the ship. Unawares. Unexpected.

And while she'd promised to give him his freedom once the treasure was returned to her, she was hoping she could convince him to return to New Providence with her, to seek a pardon. She would speak on his behalf, and she felt confident that she could convince Governor Rogers to forgive Sterling's pirating ways.

She certainly had.

He'd been a product of his surroundings: follow orders or risk death.

He was a pirate only because he'd been living on a pirate ship. In his heart, he was as honest as the other men rowing in this boat. There was a goodness in him.

She believed that with all her heart.

The prow of the boat knocked up against the *Phantom Mist* The sailor in the lead stood and swung a grappling hook. It landed with a thud. Before she knew what was happening, Sterling was scrambling up it like a monkey. He disappeared over the top.

Suddenly, Jacob's ladders were being tossed over the side. The men were taking advantage, using the rope ladders to climb. Annalisa did the same.

She made her way up the ladder,

concentrating on how far she had to climb rather than how far she'd fall. When she got near the top, hands reached over, grabbed her, and pulled her onto the deck.

Sterling wrapped his hand around hers and tugged her toward the stern.

"I've already taken care of the man at the helm. Let's get to Crimson before he discovers we're about."

They ran up the steps to the quarterdeck. Sterling pulled open a door. Rushed inside.

Crimson had taken the entire space for his quarters. He was sitting behind his desk. He came to his feet. "Sterling?"

Holding the barrel of his gun, Sterling quickly struck him on the head with the butt. Crimson slumped to the floor.

"Why did you do that?" Annalisa asked.

"It'll be easier to transport him." He pulled rope from pockets she didn't even know he had. He tied Crimson's hands behind his back. Then he stuffed his bandanna in Crimson's mouth.

"Why?"

"So he can't call out to the men." He looked up at her from his crouched position. "Don't you know anything about pirating, Anna?"

Before she could respond, she heard distant shouting.

"The crew's been alerted," Sterling said, coming to his feet.

At that moment, a burly man barreled into the room. He wasn't wearing a red scarf around his arm. He wasn't one of theirs. And obviously, he recognized that they weren't one of his.

He drew his sword, swung it —

Annalisa felt as though she was watching someone else lift her sword to ward off the killing blow.

Steel rang against steel, but it wasn't her cutlass that had deflected the blow. It was Sterling's that met the one coming toward her. She backed up quickly, giving them room to maneuver.

"James Sterling! Thought ye be dead," the man said as he rounded his cutlass.

Sterling met it. "You thought wrong."

The men circled. Thrust. Parried. Circled.

Annalisa climbed on the desk. She spied a large rock on the corner of the desk. A strange item for a pirate to have. Still, she picked it up, and when the pirate came near she conked him on the head. He went down like an anchor tossed into the sea.

"Good work," Sterling said, helping her down.

"Why did Crimson Kelly have a rock on his desk?"

"A bit of England. He always kept it with him." Sterling shrugged before kneeling down to tie up the man she'd knocked unconscious.

By the time Sterling and Annalisa returned to the quarterdeck, the crew of the *Phantom Mist* had been subdued. She didn't spot any lifeless bodies. Had there been no casualties? Could they have been that fortunate?

She was grateful to see Nathaniel standing there, tall, straight, issuing orders. "Get the captives into the hold. We'll lock them in there for the time being."

"Nathaniel, how many men did we lose?"

He turned to Annalisa. "None. The cowards surrendered straightaway. Did you get Crimson Kelly?"

Annalisa nodded. "Sterling knocked him out. He's in his quarters unconscious and trussed up like a holiday pig, along with another fellow."

"Good. Kane, take Sterling's weapons."

"I don't think so," Sterling said, and Annalisa heard the warning in his voice.

"Your job is done here, Sterling. Surrender your weapons," Nathaniel ordered.

"If you want them, take them."

Nathaniel's sword sang as he pulled it from his scabbard. "If I must."

"Nathaniel —"

"Let it be, Anna," Sterling said quietly. He withdrew his sword. "This is between Northrup and me. It has nothing to do with him not trusting me." He snaked his arm around her, pulled her close, and planted a quick kiss on her lips. "It's about you."

Then he abruptly released her and jumped down to the main deck. "Isn't that right, *Mr. Northrup?*"

His tone was mocking, the address not one of respect.

"You've been nothing but trouble ever since we took you captive," Nathaniel said.

"Trouble? I led you to the island. The ship came just as I predicted. I organized the assault, during which you lost not a man. I daresay the outcome would have been much different had we followed your plan. What more would you have of me to prove my worth?"

With swords pointed at each other, they slowly began to circle.

"I would have you drop your weapon and surrender."

"I promised him his freedom!" Annalisa yelled.

The men had seen to the prisoners, dispatching them all belowdecks and closing the hatch on them. Now they were gathering around to watch the spectacle.

"I promised him nothing," Nathaniel said.

He lunged, cutting his sword through the air. It sang a tune of destruction.

Annalisa gasped at the swiftness of his motion.

But Sterling was more than ready. He blocked Nathaniel's sword with his own. Steel rasped against steel as the men broke apart and rebalanced their stances.

They circled a bit more. Then Sterling pounced.

This was nothing like what she'd practiced.

It was fast, brutal, ferocious, with each man slashing at the other. Sterling ducked to avoid a blow. Nathaniel jumped back to miss a deadly thrust.

Then they were attacking again. Hard clashes, the vibrating steel echoing through the night. She could only imagine the jarring that their arms were taking.

The one thing she was grateful for was that they were well matched. Still, it seemed insane for them to be fighting . . . over her. Surely there was more to it than that.

She'd always suspected that Nathaniel fancied her. And she liked him immensely. But what she felt for Sterling . . .

She couldn't deny that her heart leaped into her throat each time Nathaniel lunged for Sterling. She didn't want either man hurt, but if one had to lose, God help her, she wanted it to be Nathaniel. Secretly, she was rooting for Sterling. Wanting him to be victorious. She wanted to share the spoils of this adventure with him. She wanted to give him his freedom, but she wanted it to lead him back to her.

Sterling and Nathaniel were cautiously circling each other now. Then Nathaniel moved past the main mast, obviously in retreat. Not a very wise action when your opponent was a pirate.

Suddenly, a heavy netting fell on top of Sterling, dropping him to the deck. He lost the grip on his sword and it clattered at his feet.

Nathaniel quickly stepped forward and kicked it beyond reach.

Annalisa wanted to shout, "Not fair!"

Nathaniel had obviously set the trap and lured Sterling into it.

"James Sterling, by order of the royal governor of New Providence, you are under arrest," Nathaniel declared.

Annalisa hurried down to the main deck. "Nathaniel, what are you doing?"

"I know your marque is forged, Anna. Mine isn't. I have the governor's endorsement on this little expedition to put an end to piracy on the high seas. He granted pardons. All who didn't renounce piracy at the time are fair game. I'm declaring them all my prisoners. I'm taking control of the ships."

"You knew about my forged marque but you said nothing?"

"I lacked a ship, you lacked a crew. I think we both gained here, and I knew from the beginning Sterling wouldn't cooperate with me. We needed the information he possessed to accomplish our mission: to capture Crimson Kelly and regain the treasure."

"You used me."

"I did what I must for king and country." He

swung around. "Clap him in irons and deliver him along with Crimson Kelly to the brig of *The Dangerous Lady*."

The netting was thrown off and Sterling was jerked to his feet.

"We're not finished here, Northrup," Sterling said.

Annalisa felt a swelling in her heart at the sight of him standing proud and defiant.

"I disagree. We won't bother with shackles in the brig as you'll only undo them. They say fifty lashes will kill a man, so I'll spare you that final lash. Forty-nine is all you'll receive, tomorrow morning and every morning until the treasure is recovered. Sleep well, Sterling," Nathaniel said.

Annalisa watched with helplessness as Sterling was dragged away.

"Don't look so desolate, Anna," Nathaniel said. "We're both after the same thing. The treasure. Your father's life depends on it. Or have you forgotten?"

She shook her head. "No, I haven't forgotten."

"As long as we're not working at cross-purposes, you may remain captain of *The Dangerous Lady* and sail her to New Providence.

I spoke true when I told you that I thought you could handle her. I've never known a lady I think more highly of," he said.

"You're not really going to take a cat-o'-nine to his back again, are you?"

"If I must. But I doubt I'll have to. Rather poor planning on Sterling's part to knock Crimson Kelly out. It delays us getting what we want. Once Crimson awakens, we'll see if we can convince him to tell us where he buried the treasure."

"Sterling told me that grog loosens his tongue."

Nathaniel smiled, no doubt because he saw she was willing to cooperate. "Then we'll treat him to some grog. Are we in agreement that we shall continue to work together?"

"By all means. Once we've finished up here, come to my cabin so we might toast our new — and honest — partnership."

# CHAPTER ELEVEN

James took the bent nail he'd hidden in a plank in the corner of the cell a few days earlier and worked it in the lock of his cell. He'd long ago learned to trust no one save himself. When the crewmen escorted him down here, he'd headed to the cell on the left without complaint. And they'd not objected to him choosing his own quarters for the duration of the journey.

He heard a groan and a mumbling in the cell next to his. Crimson had been tossed unceremoniously into it by his captors. James had hoped his former captain would sleep until James made his own escape but apparently that was not to be.

"Well, Sterling, this is a bloody mess you've managed to get us into this time."

James didn't glance over as Crimson came to stand by the bars separating their cells.

"I see you're up to your usual tricks," Crimson said.

"Nice to see you again, Crimson, but I won't be staying for tea."

Crimson laughed heartily. "Still mad at me, boy?"

"You marooned me."

"Aye, but I sent a ship by to rescue ye."

"Six months later? I could have been dead by then."

"I was just trying to teach ye a lesson. Ye don't keep the spoils from yer captain. When we get out of here, I'll make ye first mate."

James heard the lock click, and it opened. He removed it, then pushed open the door. It creaked on its hinges.

He held up the nail. "Sorry, matey, but the key only works in the lock on my door." He tossed it to the distant corner and sent several rats scurrying.

"Now, James, lad, what kind of friend are ye to be abandoning me like this?"

"We were never friends, Crimson."

"They'll stretch me neck, matey."

"Maybe it deserves to be stretched."

"You always had a weak stomach for the killing."

James touched his fingers to his forehead in a mock salute. "So long, Crimson. Good luck to you."

"We'll meet again, matey!" Crimson called after him as James dashed up the steps. "I swear to you, we will."

Somehow James didn't doubt it.

At the top of the stairs, he stopped, listened, heard nothing. He slipped out onto the deck. He saw no one keeping watch on this ship, no one on the other. Odd. Maybe they were on the other side.

But bless 'em, they'd moored the *Phantom Mist* to *The Dangerous Lady*. Both bobbed side by side in the water, their hulls almost touching.

"Ferret?" he called out, his voice low.

"Aye, Cap'n," came to him from the dark.

"Where are the lookouts?"

"I took care of 'em. Only need one arm to deliver a good conk to the skull."

"Good man. Weapons?"

"I watched 'em like you told me to do. They didn't bring the weapons over from the *Phantom Mist*."

"Very good. I'd say we're all set. Let's go."

James removed his boots and slipped them into the sack Ferret held out to him. In bare feet, he crept across the deck, making not a single sound. At the railing, he swung over, grabbing hold of the thick rope mooring the two ships together. He threw his legs up and crossed his feet over the rope. Then he began sliding, hand over hand, hanging down, his back to the water, toward the *Phantom Mist*.

He'd spent a good part of his life climbing rigging. This was no hard task.

When he got to the other ship, he went over the side, landing soundlessly on her deck. He waited, looking, holding his breath, listening. Maybe Northrup was daft enough to think no guards were needed here, with the prisoners in the hold.

On the balls of his feet, he made his way quickly along the side of the ship. He lifted the planking used for disembarking at docks and put it into position, scooting it across to form a walkway between the two ships. He watched as Ferret scurried across like the creature he was named after.

"Get the men out of the hold," James ordered.

Ferret left to see to his task. James hurried to the helm.

And there she was, stepping out of the shadows in much the same way she'd stepped out of the fog in Nouvelle-Orléans.

"I see you figured out how to pick the lock on the cell door," she said quietly. "Although I suspected that you always knew."

He quickly looked around, but there was no one else in sight. She was either very brave or very foolish. Brave, he decided.

"Your Mr. Northrup wouldn't approve of you being here," he said.

"Mr. Northrup came to my cabin and was met with a bottle of wine."

"He's drunk?"

"No, I didn't pour it. I hit him on the head with it."

He couldn't help himself. He smiled. And then he grew somber.

"Are you going to try to stop me, Anna?"

"No. I gave you my word that I'd grant you your freedom. I intend to keep it."

"Then you should get off the ship. I plan to set sail immediately, before my escape is discovered."

She took a step nearer. "Don't go."

**171**

"I've no choice, Anna. I'll hang otherwise."

"Not necessarily. Generally, they only hang the captain."

"Not anymore. They're making an example of all pirates. They hang us, tar us, and cage our corpses in iron gibbets to rot. I'd rather die with a sword in my hand and the wind at my back."

"I'll speak on your behalf."

He couldn't help himself. He reached out and touched her cheek. "And what would you say?"

"That you're not a pirate at heart."

Slowly, he skimmed his thumb over her lips. "You're wrong, Anna. I *am* a pirate. I'll always be a pirate. I love this life more than anything. The one thing I've always lacked is a ship to call my own." He looked about. "And now I have it."

"Cap'n?"

He dropped his hand to his side. "Yes, Mr. Ferret?"

"What be yer orders?"

"Prepare to set sail, quickly and quietly."

"And what of 'er?"

"Captain Townsend will be returning to her

ship." Without another word, he took her hand and led her to where he'd set up the plank for Ferret. "It's sturdy enough. You can hurry across."

"Just like that? Not even the courtesy of a good-bye?"

"I've never been one for saying good-bye." Perhaps because he'd never before had someone to say good-bye to.

"I'm giving you a ship," she pointed out tartly.

He grinned. "No, I'm *taking* it."

"In either case, I should get something in return. It's the pirate way." She placed her hands on either side of his face, leaned in, and kissed him.

It was the sweetest of kisses. It spoke volumes. It told of moments shared, memories made, and things between them that could never be . . . but would never be forgotten.

She leaned back and smiled. "A fair trade, pirate."

It seemed an eternity had passed since he'd spoken similar words to her in the hold of a ship. At that time, he'd thought he'd never see her again. This time, he *knew*, beyond any doubt, he'd never see her again. He swallowed hard, surprised by how unappealing the notion was. But he couldn't stray from his course.

"Indeed, a fair trade, m'lady."

He wanted to pull her to him, wanted to keep her there, aboard his ship. Instead, he held her steady and helped her climb onto the planking. He watched as she scurried across it, her skirt dancing around her bare ankles.

A gentleman would look away . . .

But as he'd proven, he was no gentleman.

When she was safely on the deck of the other ship, he pulled back the planking.

"Weigh anchor and make for the high seas, Mr. Ferret."

"Aye, Cap'n. Come along, me hearties, step lively now."

The sails were unfurled. James heard them capturing the wind. He heard the grinding as the anchor was hoisted.

It was harder than he'd expected it to be to turn his back and head to the helm, but he did. The *Phantom Mist* was his ship now. He wouldn't consider the cost.

As it sailed past *The Dangerous Lady*, he glanced back to see Anna still standing on the deck. She was more dangerous than he realized, in ways he'd not anticipated.

But not even for her would he risk a hanging.

Annalisa watched the ship slip through the waters like a ghostly phantom. Only when she could no longer see its captain did she turn and make her way to her own cabin.

Opening the door, she stepped inside. She was greeted with a grunting and a scraping of a chair across the floor, its occupant extremely unhappy. Not that she blamed him. Although, in truth, she felt he'd gotten what he deserved. He'd taken her by surprise on the *Phantom Mist*. So she'd taken him by surprise here. She'd knocked him out, and with Kane's help she'd secured him to the chair.

"Relax, Nathaniel." She pulled her knife from its scabbard. She walked around behind him and cut his bindings.

He leaped to his feet and snatched the scarf out of his mouth. "You let him escape, didn't you?"

"I gave him my word."

While watching Sterling leave had hurt more than she realized possible, she was not about to go back on her word.

"He had a reward on his head. And that ship —" Nathaniel began.

"This ship will become yours once we've completed our task. I gave you my word. You can't expect me to keep it to you and not to Sterling."

"You and I had an arrangement."

"Yes. I'm captain of this ship until we regain the treasure and free my father. To that end, we need to speak with Crimson Kelly in order to discover where on this wretched island he's buried the treasure. Let's see if he's awake and agreeable to giving us the information we need."

She knew Nathaniel was angry with her, but his anger would diminish in time.

"He's not going to tell us simply because we ask," Nathaniel grumbled as they made their way down the stairs.

"We'll see."

Crimson Kelly was awake, sitting in the corner of the cell. He slowly came to his feet. "Well, well, well. I thought ye'd be paying me a visit sooner or later."

Oxford educated? He hardly sounded it, and while she was tempted to tell him that she knew all about his playacting, she had more pressing matters on her mind. If he wanted to act, let him.

"I'm Annalisa Townsend. You stole an ivory chest of treasure from the *Horizon* more than a year ago. I'm here to reclaim it."

"I take so much plunder. Surely ye don't expect me to remember particulars."

"You burned the ship."

"I burn all ships."

"I was on board."

"Ah," he said, moving his finger through the air. "Now, ye I'd remember." His grin broadened. "Ye wouldn't be the lass who gave Sterling that useless trinket he wears on his finger as a reminder of his foolishness, now would ye?"

She angled her chin. "I would."

"I marooned him for that bit of stupidity." He grimaced. "He took it poorly. Never did have a sense of humor, that lad."

"So now you remember the ship?" Anna asked.

"Aye."

"And the chest?"

"Aye."

"Where did you bury it?" Anna asked, getting right to the point.

"Bury it? How's a pirate to spend treasure if it's buried, I ask ye?"

"Everyone knows you bury your treasure on this island. That you blind men and leave them here to wander until they die. That their souls cry out mournfully —"

"Now who told ye that bit of rubbish? James Sterling?" he asked before she could answer. "The lad always did have an active imagination."

"I heard about you burying your treasure long before I crossed paths with Sterling again. They say you have no maps; that the burial places are all in your head."

He laughed. "In my head? Exactly." He twirled his finger in a circle. "The rumors about me burying me treasure are only a bit of misleading gossip that goes around. People tear up me island from time to time lookin' fer it — when they've the good sense to figure out which one it is. They'll never find it here, because I keep it in a hidey-hole on me ship. But since the legend of Crimson Kelly says I bury it, no one tears me ship apart looking for it."

"You're lying," Annalisa snarled. "You'll tell me where it is or you'll know the taste of the cat."

"No need to threaten me, lass. Ask James Sterling. He can tell ye where it be."

Annalisa was struck too dumb to speak.

Nathaniel wasn't. "Sterling has escaped, taking your ship with him. Are you saying he knows where the hidey-hole is?"

"'Course he does. 'Twas his idea, after all. Helped me build it, he did." He leered through the space between the bars. "But I'm thinking he didn't tell you that."

# CHAPTER TWELVE

Annalisa stood on the deck, staring out into the blackness of the night. Nothing was visible except the ocean and a star-filled sky. No phantom silhouettes. No ship on the horizon.

The *Phantom Mist* and its new captain had disappeared like smoke in a breeze. She could picture Sterling standing at the helm with the wind billowing the sails of his ship, billowing the sleeves of his shirt.

*"I'm a pirate, Anna. I'll always be a pirate."*

She hadn't believed the words when Sterling had spoken them. Hadn't wanted them to be true.

She'd thought Crimson Kelly was ruthless. But Sterling was more ruthless, more underhanded, more treacherous. She couldn't think of enough words to describe her vile dislike of him. He stole from those he knew. Worse, he'd stolen knowing what the cost would be to her.

"Do you want me to have the men make sail?" Nathaniel said quietly from behind her.

"Which direction?" she asked listlessly.

"You know him, Anna. Where would he head?"

"Where he won't be found."

"If it eases whatever you're feeling, I think this was his plan all along. You'd commented how easily we'd captured him. And that weasel fellow —"

"Ferret," she said softly.

"He's gone as well."

She nodded, sighed, swiped at an irritating tear. She was trying to hold them back, but they were slowly escaping, rolling down her cheek one by one.

"Surely Crimson Kelly can help us find them," Nathaniel said.

She heard the encouragement in his voice. Was grateful for his optimism.

"We'll make plans on the morrow," she said.

"Very good. And when we find him, leave him to me. He'll tell me where the treasure is hidden."

"I doubt it."

"Then we'll take the ship apart. Plank by plank."

She slowly shook her head. "The first thing he'll do is rid himself of the treasure."

"Even now, then, he could be on the other side of the island burying it."

"He'll get far away from us as quickly as possible."

"Devil take him."

"I suspect he shall when the time comes."

Nathaniel cleared his throat. "I'm sorry I didn't tell you about my letter of marque. I'd planned to use it only if we were ever boarded and in danger of being arrested."

"I forged one only because I didn't think you or a crew would follow me without one. I feel as though I'm no better than a pirate, lying to my crew, doing whatever is necessary to gain what I want."

"You're nothing like a pirate."

They could debate this matter all night. She wasn't in the mood. She needed time alone, and she knew the only way to acquire it was to give Nathaniel something of importance to occupy him. "I've changed my mind. Go ahead and have the men unfurl the mainsail. I'm ready to put some distance between us and this wretched island."

"That's the daring girl I know, Anna. When we find Sterling, he'll rue the day he ever crossed paths with us."

Leaving her side, he began shouting orders. The men jumped to obey. It wasn't long before she heard the wind slapping at the sails, felt the breeze rushing past as they headed out into deeper waters.

She would find James Sterling. No matter how long it took. No matter how much it cost her personally. And this time, she'd show him no mercy.

He'd done more than steal the treasure. He'd stolen her heart.

The treasure was exactly where James had known it would be. Behind a false wall. A hollowed-out space, hidden behind shelves where Crimson kept his precious books. For all his blustering and crudity, his embracing of the pirate life, he loved reading. Once Crimson told James that he considered his books more valuable than the treasure they hid, but he needed the treasure to purchase the books.

James had never understood that philosophy.

Gold, silver, jewels . . . they offered a man security. They provided everything a man could ever want. If his mother had possessed no more than a handful, she'd have never been forced to give him up. She'd have had the means to feed him, to provide for him. He'd have lived a very different life.

Would it have been a life he'd have embraced? Would he have known where the stars in the sky fell to earth? Would he have known laughter so lyrical that the memory of it made him smile?

If he'd never been on the sea, he'd have never met Anna.

He stood at Crimson's desk, looking at the ivory chest. It was smaller than he remembered. Two feet wide, perhaps a foot and a half in depth. Easily hidden. Easily found.

He skimmed his fingers over the top of the chest. Engraved in copper was the royal coat of arms. This chest had been entrusted to the care of Anna's father. It was the chest she'd searched for. And inside was the treasure she'd sacrificed for.

While he'd known only a few true ladies in his life, he'd known many women, but not one of them had Anna's determination, drive, and willingness to do what was needed to achieve her goal. She'd almost succeeded.

Her failure had come in trusting him.

He shrugged off the guilt that pricked his conscience. She was the one who'd given her word that she'd grant his freedom. He'd never given his word that he wouldn't attempt to escape. He was a pirate. She'd simply forgotten that he wasn't honorable.

Although he couldn't deny that he'd done all in his power to make her forget. He'd charmed her, with deliberation, knowing that she would fall for him.

What he hadn't expected was to fall for her.

Devil take her! He didn't like the way he felt whenever he thought of her. Ashamed, as though he'd done something wrong. He'd done only what any self-respecting pirate would do. He'd sought out the treasure, and he'd taken it.

He'd done it without any loss of life. She should be grateful for that. It was a kindness. The treasure was simply his reward.

He loosened the latch on the chest. Crimson had long ago broken the lock and looked inside. Slowly, James lifted the lid and peered at the contents.

A slow smile spread across his face. He dipped his hands as though slipping them into the water of the cove to capture a starfish. He lifted his hands, his palms filled with gold coins. They slipped through his fingers, clinking as they fell and hit the coins that remained inside.

He grabbed the bottle of rum waiting for him on the corner of the desk. He brought the half-empty bottle to his lips and gulped some more. It dulled the ache in his chest, an ache he didn't understand. It was as though someone had pierced it with a sword.

He dropped into the chair and drank until the bottle was empty. Then he tossed it against the far wall. It hit hard and shattered. That was jolly stupid. Now if he tried to go to bed, he'd cut his feet.

He'd go out to the deck and look at the stars — but they'd remind him of Anna. He wanted no reminders.

Leaning forward, he sifted his fingers through the coins again.

So many coins, so much wealth.

At long last he had it all: the ship, the treasure, a crew to follow him.

Twisting the ring on his little finger, he wondered why he felt as though he'd gained nothing.

## CHAPTER THIRTEEN

The wind filled the sails and the ship sliced through the water. Annalisa felt the excitement thrumming through her veins. She was once again the predator instead of the prey.

That morning she had ordered the crew to dump overboard any refuse, anything that they could do without. A lighter ship could move more swiftly, and right now speed was of the essence.

At dawn, she'd stood on the quarterdeck, looking through her spyglass, when she caught sight of a ship on the distant horizon. It had to be the *Phantom Mist*. She had little doubt that Sterling had sailed through the night.

He'd know that Annalisa would soon learn of his betrayal. And if he'd learned nothing else about her, he'd have learned that she'd be diligent in her pursuit of him. She wouldn't let him escape easily.

And this time, she wouldn't succumb to his charms. She'd deliver the pirate to New Providence for justice. He'd spend the journey in the hold. Shackled. Locked in a cell. With two guards standing watch at all times. He'd survive on bread and water. If he survived at all.

Mayhaps she'd even let Nathaniel have the satisfaction of starting Sterling's day with a taste of the cat. Perhaps she'd wield the lash herself. She was a woman scorned, and she didn't much care for it.

Several times since they'd departed she'd looked back at the island, but a fog had come up and all she saw was mist. It was for the best. She didn't want to remember what she considered paradise.

"Sterling won't surrender easily," Nathaniel said speculatively beside her.

"It might not even be him," she said, surprised to discover that the possibility gave her a sense of relief. For all the harsh thoughts she harbored toward him, a part of her didn't want to exact revenge.

"The odds are it is."

"It could be another ship."

"You say that as though you're hoping it is."

She glanced over at Nathaniel. "So many of our crewmen are still recovering from last night's adventure. I'm not certain they're up to another confrontation so soon."

"It's personal now, Anna. They're up to it. Besides, we took them with hardly any skirmishes."

She heard the bitterness in his voice. Not that she blamed him. Sterling had duped them all and sprung the last trap.

"I don't want him killed," she said.

"We may have no choice in the matter."

"Nathaniel —"

"I'll not risk my life or that of my crew to keep him alive." He sighed deeply. "Neither will I kill him if it's not necessary. But he's fallen for two of our traps now. I don't know if I can set a third."

"Mayhaps we can parley, convince him to return the ivory chest."

He scoffed. "If he was going to give it to you, he'd have given it to you before he set sail."

She couldn't deny the truth of his words. Sterling had known the treasure was aboard the ship, and he'd not said a word to her. She suspected he wanted the treasure more than the ship.

"The ship's turnin', Cap'n!" her lookout called from above.

Annalisa lifted the spyglass to her eye. "It appears to be turning this way."

"He must think meeting us head-on will give him a tactical advantage."

She peered harder through the spyglass. "It's not the *Phantom Mist*. The figurehead is wrong." She watched as the ship's colors were raised. Beside her, Nathaniel grunted.

"Black flag," he muttered. "Not Crimson's red. And what is that symbol? A pirate and a . . . what is it?"

"Death," Annalisa said bleakly. Her stomach dropped to her toes as she lowered her spyglass. "It's Black Bart Roberts."

"We can try to outsail him," Nathaniel said, his voice scratchy as though his mouth had suddenly gone dry.

She watched the speed with which *Royal Fortune* moved over the sea. "I think we'd do better to prepare for battle."

"It's said he has captured four hundred ships."

"Then let's do what we can do ensure it's not four hundred and one."

"If we surrender, he might show mercy."

"Sterling told me the man is the most fiercesome pirate on the seas. Mercy is not in his character."

"Sterling also told you that Crimson Kelly buried his treasure."

"He had no reason to lie about this pirate," she told him. "And we're wasting precious time talking."

"You're quite right. If we capture him, he will make quite the prize to deliver to Governor Rogers."

"Roberts you need not take care not to kill," she said.

He nodded, before turning around and shouting, "All hands! Prepare for battle!"

There was a scurrying about the ship the likes of which she'd never seen. The powder monkeys and several of the crew hurried down to the gun deck. They only had fourteen cannons, but they would have to do. They had swivel guns up top.

"They won't want to destroy the ship," Nathaniel said. "If they fire volleys, it'll just be to unsettle us. They'll do all they can to board us. We must be prepared for close combat."

He pulled Annalisa near. She could see the concern, worry, and fear in his eyes.

"You would be safer in the hold," he said quietly.

She quickly shook her head. "My place is here with the men."

"Anna, it's different to parry against a man who has no plans to kill you. It's very different indeed to run a man through."

"I will not hide," she insisted.

"Then at least do what you can to hide the fact that you're a woman, or fighting you will be the last thing they consider."

She nodded brusquely and darted across the deck. She raced up the steps to the quarterdeck, down the short hallway, and into her cabin. Quickly, she changed into breeches and a loosely flowing shirt. She slid her braid down the back of her shirt. By the time anyone noticed it, maybe the fighting would be over.

She angled a belt across her chest and slipped in two pistols, ready to be fired. Around her waist, she tightened another belt that held her cutlass in its scabbard, and a knife.

She took a deep breath and tried to remember everything James had taught her. She could do this. She could fight to the death if she had to.

She heard a loud bang in the hallway. Dear Lord! Were they here already?

With her sword drawn, she crossed the cabin and swung open the door, only to find her way barred by stacked crates.

"Sorry, Anna!" Nathaniel called out. "It's for your own protection."

"Nathaniel, let me out!"

"When we're —"

A loud boom sounded! The ship shook. Annalisa hit the floor. She pounded her fist against the floor. She was trapped.

Another boom echoed. She heard wood splintering.

"No, no, no!"

She scrambled to her feet. She shoved on the crates. They budged not an inch. They were so heavy. Why hadn't the men tossed them overboard?

*Boom! Boom! Boom!*

The ship shuddered. She could hear men yelling and screaming. She could hear swords clashing. The pirates were here!

If she couldn't move the blasted crates, she could dismantle them. She pried the cutlass between the slats and worked a slat free. Then another. She could see what was in the crate now. Straw and . . .

Bottles of rum.

She cursed the men for holding on to their precious liquor. She dare not toss the bottles out, lest she break them and then have to deal with the glass. But she did begin working quickly to empty the crate, to lighten it.

When she had its contents scattered on the floor, she began to shove the crate to the side, inch by agonizing inch. When she'd created a wide enough crevice, she hurried to the table, grabbed a chair, and dragged it to the door. She climbed onto the chair, then onto the crate, and wiggled through the narrow opening. She dropped through to the other side and raced toward the door.

A man barged through. He swung low. She met his cutlass high, crouched, and jabbed her knife into him. Clutching his now bloodstained side, he crumpled to the floor. She darted past and out onto the quarterdeck, into the misty morning. The fog that had been surrounding the island had caught up to them. Madness and mayhem abounded.

From out of nowhere, another man seemed to appear. She deflected each parry and thrust, forcing him back, until she was able to shove him off the quarterdeck with a push of her foot. He landed hard on the main deck.

She hurried down the steps, avoiding blows, crouching, shifting from side to side, remembering everything Sterling had taught her about fighting aboard a ship. Rounding the corner, she nearly rammed into a tall, slender man dressed as though he should be in a drawing room, not aboard a ship.

"What have we here?" he asked.

Annalisa didn't have time for small talk. With her cutlass, she swung at him. His sword met hers and he laughed.

"Fiesty wench."

So much for Nathaniel's thought that breeches would disguise her gender — although she realized now his true purpose had been to get her off the deck.

Backing up, she struck again. The pirate did little more than smile as steel met steel. Then he began to swing hard and fast. Annalisa ducked and parried, but she feared she was no match for the ruthlessness of this man.

Each time she moved out of his way, he followed, quickly, with faster and faster swings of his cutlass. She knew he was trying to corner her, and she knew she'd be doomed if he succeeded, but there seemed to be nowhere else for her to go except backward.

Then her hips hit the railing. His sword struck hers with such force that her hand went numb. Her cutlass clattered on the deck.

"Surrender," he ordered.

She angled up her chin. "Never. I'll never surrender to a pirate."

"A pity." His expression turned hard; all teasing was over. He swung with such force, she knew the blow would be a killer —

*Clash!*

Suddenly, a cutlass was before her eyes, preventing the other from striking her. Nathaniel!

She shifted her gaze to the side.

"You seem to be in a spot of bother here," Sterling said.

"James."

"You've never called me that before," he

said with a grunt as he shoved the attacker's sword away.

"James Sterling," the pirate said slowly as though he were savoring fine wine. "I'd heard you were dead."

"You heard wrong, Roberts."

Annalisa felt her knees grow weak. She'd been fighting the notorious Black Bart Roberts? And lived to tell about it!

Not yet, she realized as Roberts swung his cutlass at Sterling. The vibrating clang echoed over the ship. Annalisa ducked down, retrieved her sword, and came up swinging.

Together she and Sterling were able to put Black Bart on the defensive. He was skilled, very skilled, warding off each of their thrusts.

"What of Crimson Kelly?" Black Bart asked as they continued to parry.

"He's in the brig," Sterling responded as though talking with an old friend.

"So this ship is a pirate hunter?"

"Its captain is, yes. Rather bad planning on your part to attack her. The only thing of value aboard her is her rum."

"I don't drink the devil's brew."

"So I've heard, which gives you no reason to stay."

"On the contrary, I love a good fight."

He gave them a grin so wide that Annalisa thought his jaw would come unhinged. When he stepped back, two other pirates stepped in front of him. And it was no longer she and Sterling working together to fight one man, but each of them desperately fighting their own opponent.

Annalisa knew it probably wasn't fair, but then Sterling had taught her that pirates didn't fight fair. With her left hand, she drew out a pistol and fired. The man dropped to the deck, groaning.

She pulled out her other pistol and took down the pirate fighting James. They both swung around, searching for Roberts. He was nowhere to be found.

"Pity you didn't use the pistols when Roberts was around," Sterling said.

"I forgot about them," she said honestly. She'd been so terrified it was a wonder she could think at all. "What are you doing here?"

"We were following behind you, in the fog. Didn't I warn you about Roberts?"

"You were behind us?"

"Aye." He nodded. "We pulled up alongside you to offer assistance."

It was only then she noticed that her ship was wedged between the two mighty pirate ships.

"Why? Why do you care? I know the treasure's aboard your ship. I know you knew it. Why —"

Before she could complete another of a thousand questions, someone charged him. Sterling met the combatant, swords flashing. He quickly dispensed with the fellow.

The ship suddenly listed to the side. Annalisa was saved from slipping when Sterling caught her arm.

"Your ship is badly damaged. It took cannon fire to the hull."

She heard a noise that sounded as though a tree had been felled in a forest.

"You must get aboard the *Phantom Mist* before it's too late," Sterling warned.

"Not without my crew."

"You are sorely testing my patience," he said.

"I didn't ask you to come to my rescue."

An expression she couldn't read crossed his face.

"Give the order to abandon ship," he said.

She shook her head. "It can't be that badly —"

The ship shuddered violently. This time she did lose her footing and slammed to the deck. It was going down.

"Abandon ship!" she yelled, scrambling to her feet.

James grabbed a passing seaman. "Spread the word. Get aboard the *Phantom Mist* as quickly as possible."

James turned back to her and held out his hand. "Let's go."

"No, I'm the captain. I don't leave the ship until every crewman is safely off."

"This isn't the bloody British navy! There's no one to hold you accountable."

"There's me," she said quietly. "But a pirate wouldn't understand that."

Before he could respond, she turned, searching for her men, ordering them to abandon ship. It seemed Roberts was giving the same order from the safety of his own ship because the fighting had ceased and men were scrambling to get aboard the two ships bumping against *The Dangerous Lady*.

Annalisa hurried over the deck, helping the

wounded get to the railing so they could scramble over to the *Phantom Mist*, moored to the side of her ship. She saw Sterling doing the same thing.

She swung around. The crew of the *Royal Fortune* had cut their moorings. The ship was drifing away. She had managed to survive an encounter with Black Bart.

She jerked around. "Sterling! Crimson Kelly is in the brig."

"I'll get him." He disappeared into the hold.

She was surprised by how swiftly the men were able to get off the ship. Soon she was the only one standing on the deck. Waiting. Waiting for Sterling. He wasn't a member of her crew. She supposed she had no obligation to wait for him.

The ship groaned with fierceness and sounded as though it was being split asunder.

"Cut the moorings!" someone yelled from the other ship.

"Anna, get over here!" It was Nathaniel, aboard the *Phantom Mist*, yelling for her.

But she couldn't leave, not yet, not without Sterling. She watched in horror as the other ship began to float away. Her own ship moaned.

Sterling appeared out of the hatch. "Crimson's gone."

"Was there anyone else?"

"No one else alive."

The ship listed to the side. She grabbed the railing. They could jump in the water and be fished out, but she remembered the captain's words when the *Horizon* sank. A ship's sinking could very well carry them to the depths of the sea.

"Climb up on the railing, Anna!" Sterling shouted.

Holding on to the rigging, she did as he ordered. He hacked at a rope attached to the top of the mast. When it was loose, he raced across the deck, leaped onto the railing, and snaked an arm around her as the ship dropped beneath them . . .

With a gasp, Annalisa clung to Sterling as they swung out over the water, across the chasm separating the ships.

He released his hold on the rigging, turning his body so when they hit the deck she landed on top of him, cushioned slightly.

Safe, they were safe.

Scrambling to her feet, she rushed to the

railing in time to see the deck of *The Dangerous Lady* swallowed by the sea. Only its mast remained visible, and she knew it, too, would soon be gone.

Looking past it, she could see the *Royal Fortune*. Standing among the men on its deck were Black Bart Roberts and Crimson Kelly, side by side as though they were old friends.

"James Sterling!" Crimson Kelly called out. "We'll meet again, matey, I promise ye!"

"I look forward to it, Crimson!"

Crimson's deep laughter could be heard echoing between the ships.

"Unfurl the sails, men!" Sterling yelled. "We need to put sea between us and the *Royal Fortune*. Set the heading for north by nor'east."

"Aye, aye, Cap'n," someone said.

Annalisa turned. It was only then that she noticed her men were in the center of the deck, on their knees, not a single weapon among them. She spun back around. "What's the meaning of this, Sterling?"

"My ship, my rules."

She watched as he walked toward the men, stopping in front of Nathaniel.

"On your feet, Northrup."

Nathaniel stood, defiance in his eyes.

Sterling smiled. "They say fifty lashes will kill a man. So I'll spare you the last one."

"Don't bother with such kindness. I can take fifty easily."

"In truth, I doubt you can take five. Mr. Lewis!"

"Aye, Cap'n." A huge chunk of a man stepped forward.

"Escort Mr. Northrup to the brig."

"Aye, Cap'n." He put his beefy hand on Nathaniel's arm. "Let's go, matey."

"If it's the last thing I do, I'll see you hanged," Nathaniel vowed.

Sterling turned his back on him, and Lewis led Nathaniel away. Annalisa had thought he'd protest, but he no doubt realized he was at a disadvantage aboard a pirate ship. His struggles would be fruitless, his efforts wasted.

"Mr. Ferret!" Sterling called out.

"Aye, Cap'n." The little weasel stepped forward.

"You have our articles?"

"Aye, Cap'n." From inside his shirt, he pulled out a rolled parchment.

"Gentlemen," Sterling said. He turned and bowed toward Annalisa. "And lady. You are aboard a pirate ship. We have articles that we follow here. You are obliged to either sign them or spend the remainder of this voyage in the brig alongside Mr. Northrup where you'll no doubt perish from listening to his long-winded rants about the evils of piracy."

A few of the men chuckled.

"Mr. Ferret, read the articles."

"Aye, Cap'n." Another man took the scroll and unfurled it so Ferret could read it.

"'Number one. If any man defraud the company of a single bit of loot, marooning will be his punishment.

"'Number two. Men are obliged to keep their pistols and cutlasses clean and fit for service.

"'Number three. To desert the ship or quarters in battle will be punished by death or marooning.

"'Number four. No striking of a fellow mate onboard ship. All quarrels are to take place on shore.

"'Number five. Each man will receive an equal share of the prize'." He nodded. "There ye have it, gents."

There was mumbling among her men.

"For those of you who are squeamish about pirating, rest assured we have no plans to seize any vessels before we reach our destination,"

Sterling said. "Once there, you may disembark and go on your merry way. Until then, you are either with us or in the brig."

Annalisa watched as, one by one, her men came forward and signed the articles, effectively identifying themselves as pirates.

"What will it be, Anna?" Sterling said quietly beside her. She'd not heard him approach.

"You're asking me to be a pirate."

"I'm asking you to honor the rules of this ship."

"And if I don't sign, you'll put me in the brig."

"Not if you give me your word that you won't mutiny."

She jerked her head around and stared at him. "You trust my word?"

"I do."

She nodded. "Then you have it. I'll not invoke a mutiny."

"Then the captain's cabin will be readied for you."

He turned and she grabbed his arm. "Please, don't take a cat to Nathaniel."

"Do you love him?"

"He's my friend and he's been a good quartermaster. Please, don't bloody his back."

"What do you take me for? A barbarian?" He touched her cheek. "I never had any intention of taking a lash to him, but neither do I want him sleeping soundly."

"I doubt any of us will sleep soundly until we're off this ship. Which port are you taking us to?"

"New Providence."

Annalisa felt her heart hammer against her ribs. "They'll hang you there."

"Probably, but we have an ivory chest filled with gold coins to deliver."

She gasped as warmth flooded her. "You were bringing the treasure back to me."

"Don't say that as though I'm a hero. It simply wasn't as much as I'd remembered. It's hardly worth the bother."

And yet he had bothered.

"Thank you."

"Words are hardly a fair trade. I want tonight, Anna, and every moment that remains before we reach New Providence."

"You shall have it."

# CHAPTER FOURTEEN

Most of the crew were belowdecks, orders of their captain. The only ones about were the lookout in the crow's nest and the helmsmen steering the ship.

In the captain's cabin, Annalisa had found a blue dress. Silk. From the orient. She didn't know how it had come to be on the ship. She was certain it was plunder. But she was grateful that for tonight she'd not have to wear the breeches.

She'd also taken a bath. As had James. She could tell because his hair was still damp at the ends when he came to her cabin and escorted her to the quarterdeck.

He'd placed a barrel of rum there and covered it with surplus sailcloth. A lantern in its center provided light. He'd brought chairs from his quarters so that they might dine by starlight.

The cook had prepared some sort of pheasant. Where he'd gotten it, she hadn't a clue. Maybe on Crimson's island. But it was delicious. Now she and James were sharing a slice of cake that tasted a good deal like rum.

"Do pirates put rum in everything?" she asked.

"Whenever possible."

"I've never eaten dinner outside," she said. In the distance, she heard the whale's song.

"If I had my druthers," James said, "I'd never go belowdecks."

She placed her elbow on the barrel and plopped her chin onto her palm. "Why?"

"I like being in the open. I think that's the reason I like the sea so much. There's nothing to confine you. Nothing to hold you in."

"I like being held," Annalisa said.

"There's a difference between being held and being confined."

"Being in the brig must have been torture for you."

"You left me a lantern. That was a kindness I'd not expected." Leaning forward, he took

**210**

her hand. "I've since learned that you're always kind."

"A few of the pirates we met today might disagree. Especially the two who felt the bite of my bullet."

He laughed. She couldn't deny how much she enjoyed the sound of his laughter.

Reaching out, she trailed her finger along the scar on his cheek. "It's a moonless night, so tell me the details, pirate."

"Shall I call up the lads out of the hold?"

Slowly she shook her head. "No."

Tonight was for them and them alone.

"Very well, then. We were sailing where the Caribbean meets the Atlantic when we saw a merchant ship, flying French colors. So we took her." He rubbed his cheek. "I was twelve, and it was the first time I boarded an enemy vessel."

"Wait a moment. If you were twelve and you're twenty-one now..." She did the calculation. "It was during Queen Anne's War. Along with Crimson, you were a privateer. You served the queen." She was stunned. How had she not managed to put it together sooner? "Little wonder you find no fault with him being a pirate."

"I never said I didn't find fault with it. I merely stated that I understood it. Now, do you want to hear the remainder of the story or not?"

"Go on," she urged.

"It was a moonless night when we attacked. We lowered two boats into the water. Because of my age, I was small, thin, fast. Like your powder monkeys. The men tossed up grappling hooks. I was the first one they sent up the rope. All I could hear was the water lapping at the boat and the ferocious pounding of my heart. I made my way up and climbed over the railing. I saw no one. I signaled the all clear. The ship creaked and moaned. It was eerie.

"I crept across the deck, and that's when the first crewman came out of hiding and attacked." He rubbed his cheek again.

"Is that how you got the scar?"

His hand stilled and he looked surprised, as though he'd not realized what he was doing. He shook his head. "That came later. Afterward, really. We thought we'd captured everyone. We were walking around the ship, another lad and I, kicking men to see if they were alive or dead. I kicked a man I was certain was dead. He grabbed my knife, the other lad screeched, the man turned to him, and I leaped between them. The knife slashed across my face."

"You saved the other boy," she said.

He shrugged. "Impossible to know. The man might not have tried to harm him, but he had bloodlust in his eyes. The next thing I knew he had a sword poking through the middle of his chest. Crimson never did take well to the dead coming back to life."

She trailed her finger along his cheek again. "You say the other lad screeched. Like a weasel?"

He grinned. "Like a ferret."

"You've known him that long?" she asked.

"Aye. Crimson took us both on about the same time. Ferret was younger, always smaller."

"You were his protector, yet he betrayed you."

James shrugged. "Odd thing is, I know if I asked, he'd die for me."

She studied him for a moment. "But you'd never ask."

"Nay. I never would."

"You're a complicated man, James Sterling," she said softly.

"Not so complicated." He stood and drew her to her feet.

She didn't hesitate to wrap her arms around his neck and to rise up on her toes. And then he was kissing her and she realized, no, he wasn't complicated at all.

With his back against the cabin wall on the quarterdeck, James held Anna in his arms, her back to his chest. He'd set a mound of blankets on the quarterdeck. She'd not objec'·d when he'd led her to them.

"I just want to watch the night with you," he'd said quietly. "And the dawn."

So now he held her, inhaling her scent, knowing what she did not fully realize.

The moments they shared before they reached New Providence were all they'd ever have. While their arrival at the port city with the treasure would herald the vindication and release of her father, for him it would result in a death sentence.

# CHAPTER FIFTEEN

"Four ninety-six, four ninety-seven, four ninety-eight" — Governor Rogers dropped the last coin into the chest — "four ninety-nine."

He glanced up at Annalisa, James, and Nathaniel. The *Phantom Mist* was so distinctive, so well known, that they'd barely spotted New Providence before two British men-of-war had descended upon them and escorted them into the harbor.

Annalisa, James, and Nathaniel had been apprehended and taken to the governor's office, despite their protests. They stood in front of his desk, having arrived that morning. Annalisa had begun to explain about her quest, but it seemed the governor already knew a good deal about it, thanks in part to the legitimate letter of marque he'd presented to Nathaniel.

Rogers, with his powdered wig sitting perfectly atop his head, looked at each of them now. "According to the king's letter, there are five hundred pieces of gold. Search the pirate," he said drolly.

One of the red-uniformed guards standing just behind them stepped forward and began to pat James's clothing.

"The king's treasurer must have miscounted," Annalisa began.

"Here 'tis." The soldier moved away from James and delivered it carefully to Rogers.

"Surely you can't fault me with wanting a small souvenir of my adventures," James said.

Rogers looked disgusted. "Lock him up."

Annalisa took a step forward. "No, please, have mercy. He saved us from Black Bart."

"Black Bart Roberts?" Rogers asked.

Annalisa nodded. "Yes, sir."

"You're telling me that you escaped the clutches of that notorious pirate?"

"With Sterling's help."

Rogers looked past her. "I didn't rescind my order, soldier. Lock him up, and bring Governor Townsend back with you."

She started to move toward James, but he held up a hand to stop her. "I'll be all right."

She wasn't so certain, but what more could she do if the governor was determined not to listen to her explanation? Not wanting to see James escorted away, she turned back to the man who held their fates in his hands. "Is my father all right?"

"You'll see for yourself soon enough." He closed the chest. "While we're waiting, tell me about these adventures of yours."

James sat in his cell brooding. They'd taken his boots, his belt, everything except his breeches and shirt. He could find nothing with which to pick a lock.

He knew that eventually he'd be brought before Governor Rogers again — to be sentenced. He knew it wouldn't go in his favor. If he'd had any chance at all for leniency, he'd lost it when he pocketed the one gold coin. How was he to know Rogers would take the time to count every blessed one?

They'd released Anna's crew, but they were holding his men aboard the ship until Rogers made time to meet with each man. He would offer them a reprieve in exchange for their word that they'd do no more pirating. Without Anna knowing, James had spoken with his men that morning, long before they'd neared New Providence. He'd encouraged them to take the offer.

As for himself, well, he was now the captain. He could hear the pronouncement: "Captain James Sterling, you'll be hanged by the neck until dead. May God have mercy on your soul."

Except James knew he was going straight to the devil.


It was three days before all the arrangements were made, before Governor Rogers allowed Annalisa to visit James. She hated to see him locked in a cell again, but she couldn't help but smile at the way he swaggered to the door as though he was about to be invited to tea.

He gave her his cocky grin. "Don't you look lovely."

She felt self-conscious in the lavender dress when they'd taken nearly everything from him. "One of the governor's assistants has a daughter about my size. I was able to borrow some of her things."

"How is your father?"

"He's lost a good bit of weight and he looks ill, but his spirits are good. Rogers believes that he had nothing to do with the thievery. He's sending us to Mourning, so my father can continue as the king wanted. A man-of-war is waiting for us in the harbor now."

"That's good. Pirates seldom attack a British man-of-war. Too many guns aboard."

The conversation was trite, meaningless. She lurched forward, wrapped her hands around the bars. They were cold. How could they be cold in the tropics?

"I tried to tell Rogers about the good things you did, but he won't believe me because of that damn forged letter of marque. He thinks I can't be trusted. And of course Nathaniel has nothing good to say about you. I'm beginning to wish you *had* taken the cat to him."

"He'll marry you if you'll have him."

"Well, I shan't have him. He's not a bad man, I know that, but neither is he . . . you."

Reaching through the bars, he touched her cheek. She turned her face into his palm.

"I told you before I'm not much for dancing," he said quietly. "I'd rather you not see me dancing the devil's jig. I suspect I won't be much good at it."

Her heart lurched and tears burned her eyes. "Surely you can escape."

"Not this time." He captured a tear that rolled down her cheek. "Don't cry. You've given me more joy than I've ever known."

"It's not enough."

He gave her a sad grin. "That's how pirates are made. The plunder we take is never enough. We're never content with what we have. We always want more."

"That's not a bad thing."

"It's time to go, miss," the guard called out.

Annalisa slammed her eyes closed. She didn't want this. She didn't want to leave him.

"I'll always be there, Anna, in every ship you see sailing past. I'll be the wind in its sails."

She squeezed her eyes tighter but couldn't stop the tears from leaking out.

"Now go, Anna."

She opened her eyes. "I love you, James Sterling, pirate that you are. Maybe you were right all along, maybe it's because you are a pirate that I love you. But I shall never forget you."

She spun around and dashed out of the room and down the hallway to the courtyard. All the while her heart was breaking.

# CHAPTER SIXTEEN

"Well, it doesn't look like much yet, but the port city will be something spectacular when we've finished building it," Annalisa's father said.

As she stood on the sandy shore beside him, she couldn't help thinking how glad she was to have him back — and she fought not to think of the cost. While she was paying with her heart, James Sterling would pay with his life. She still had a difficult time believing he was willing to sacrifice so much for her.

She glanced at her father. His pallor was no longer ashen, and he had a more lively step to his gait. He was optimistic about his new post as governor of Mourning, in spite of the fact that it didn't have a proper harbor for docking.

The British man-of-war that had brought them here had dropped anchor a ways out and used a pirogue to get them to shore. The supplies needed to be unloaded, and various preparations were required. Presently, the port city was little more than straw shacks.

"I'm going to name the city Rhiannon, in honor of your mother," her father said quietly. "She always wanted to come to the Caribbean, but she had a fear of sailing." He looked over at her. "You don't seem to have inherited her tendency to avoid being near water."

Annalisa laughed lightly. "Much to my surprise, I love being on a ship."

"Well, it'll be a while before you're on one again. We have much to do here. We'd best get to it."

Annalisa spent her days doing what she could to help her father. Carpenters arrived and work began on the city that her father had carefully mapped out. The fun in being part of a place just being built was that everything was unnamed. Her father gave her the honor of naming the roads. At present the town had three intersections at its center. She designated them Gold, Silver, and Sterling.

And every morning she began her day by

sitting atop the hill she'd named Pirate's Lookout and gazing toward the horizon, searching for ships so she could pretend that James Sterling was sailing by.

This particular morning, to her immense disappointment, a fog was rolling in. She could see the shore and the water that lapped at it, but just beyond where ships normally dropped anchor a gray mist swirled. She knew there was little point in waiting. It would be some time before the sun burned off the fog. Until then she'd see no distant ships. Yet she was reluctant to leave.

Six weeks had passed since she left New Providence. She'd received no word regarding James's fate, but she couldn't stop herself from believing that he'd already danced his jig. The one concession Governor Rogers had granted her was a promise that he would see James decently buried rather than displayed as a warning to other pirates.

"Land ho!" echoed toward her.

Then she saw the prow of a ship, its figurehead a roaring lion, coming slowly through the mist. Her heart hammered.

Even as she lifted her spyglass to her eye, she knew it wasn't James. Rogers had no doubt given the captured pirate ship to someone else. Nathaniel perhaps. He was owed a ship.

She watched as the *Phantom Mist* dropped anchor. She heard another splash, the longboat being lowered to the water. Minutes later, it emerged from the fog.

A man stood at the prow as though he was anxious to be on shore. He didn't have Nathaniel's curling blond hair. His was dark, so very dark.

Tears burned her eyes. She shook her head. It absolutely couldn't be. She was seeing a phantom, an illusion. She was seeing what her heart wanted to be true.

She brought the spyglass into focus on the man's face. It was James!

James with his dark hair caught back, his green eyes focused on the shore. The scar across his cheek that, in her eyes, only made him more handsome.

"James!"

She jumped to her feet and began racing down the hill. She nearly took a tumble a time or two before she made it to level ground. She rushed onto the sand and continued running, waving madly. "James!"

He must have heard her. He looked her way. "Anna!"

He vaulted out of the boat, landing in water up to his knees. He waded through the surf toward her at an angle that brought him to shore just as she reached him.

She flung herself into his arms, felt their strength fold around her. He was no phantom of her imagination. He was real. So real.

"You escaped!" she cried. "I knew you would. I never doubted it for a moment."

She kissed him. His scarred cheek, his nose, his chin, and finally his mouth. His wonderful teasing mouth.

When they finally broke apart, they were both breathing heavily. His eyes roamed over her face as though he wanted to memorize every line. But there was no need. He would have the opportunity to see it every day.

"I'll go with you," she said quickly. "I'll sign any articles you want me to. I'd rather be a pirate and be with you than be alone on this wretched island without you."

Laughing, he lifted her off her feet and spun her around. "Ah, Anna, I'd give you almost anything, but I can't offer you the pirating life."

When she was nearly dizzy, he stopped spinning. He cradled her face between his strong hands. "I renounced my pirating ways."

She stared at him, dumbfounded, before finally stammering, "P-p-p-ardon?"

He grinned. "Aye, 'tis true."

"But the ship. You have the ship."

"Aye. A lot of pirates still roam the sea, and Governor Rogers is offering a nice reward for their capture. And who better to catch a pirate than a pirate?"

"You're a pirate hunter now?"

He nodded. "I'd rather be a pirate hunter and have you at my side than be a pirate and sail the seas without you."

"You'll take me with you, then?"

"Why do you think I'm here, Anna?"

She hugged him tightly. "I love you, James Sterling."

"I love you, too," he whispered hoarsely. Leaning back, he gazed into her eyes. "You're the only treasure I'll ever need."

Then he was kissing her again.

This pirate whom she'd caught.

This pirate who had stolen her heart.

# GLOSSARY OF PIRATING TERMS

**Cat-o'-nine-tails:** A rope with nine cords used as a lash

**Devil rot you:** Profanity

**Gibbet:** A hanging iron cage where corpses were placed to rot as a warning

**Handsomely now:** Hurry up

**Me hearties:** My mates

**Pirogue:** A canoelike boat

**Pox take you:** Profanity

**Sea rover:** Another name for a pirate

**Swab:** Large mop made of old rope, used to clean the ship's deck

**Taste of the cat:** Refers to the cat-o'-nine-tails

**Weigh anchor:** Raise the anchor

**Yard:** Horizontal spar on a mast from which square sails are set

**Yardarm:** The outermost tips of the yard

# AUTHOR'S NOTE

Black Bart Roberts was a real pirate who sailed the African coast and the Caribbean between 1719 and 1722. His ship was *Royal Fortune*. His first flag showed him and death holding an hourglass. It is believed he attacked more than 470 ships, more than any other pirate.

New Providence was a pirate haven in the Bahamas. Its first royal governor, Woodes Rogers, was charged by King George in 1718 with ending piracy in the area. He hanged a good many pirates who refused to denounce their pirating ways. He really did believe that the best person to hunt down a pirate was a pirate, and he hired former pirates to capture those who were still looting ships or sacking coastal towns.

Nouvelle-Orléans, later to be known as New Orleans, was founded in 1718 by the French.

Queen Anne's War was fought between 1702 and 1713. The British were at war with the French. Letters of marque were issued granting privateers the right to raid enemy ships. It was an inexpensive way to build a navy. When the war ended, the marques were rescinded, and these men were no longer needed, so they turned to what they were most skilled at — raiding ships. But without their country's blessing, they were now considered pirates. It was this period in history that spawned so many infamous pirates and led to the "golden age of pirating."

**Jade Parker** is the author of many books, though this is her first about pirates. She lives near Dallas, Texas, with her husband, two sons, and two dogs.

# To Do List: Read all the Point books!

## By Aimee Friedman

- ☐ **South Beach**
  0-439-70678-5

- ☐ **French Kiss**
  0-439-79281-9

- ☐ **Hollywood Hills**
  0-439-79282-7

## By Hailey Abbott

- ☐ **Summer Boys**
  0-439-54020-8

- ☐ **Next Summer: A Summer Boys Novel**
  0-439-75540-9

- ☐ **After Summer: A Summer Boys Novel**
  0-439-86367-8

- ☐ **Last Summer: A Summer Boys Novel**
  0-439-86725-8

## By Claudia Gabel

- ☐ **In or Out**
  0-439-91853-7

## By Nina Malkin

- ☐ **6X: The Uncensored Confessions**
  0-439-72421-X

- ☐ **6X: Loud, Fast, & Out of Control**
  0-439-72422-8

- ☐ **Orange Is the New Pink**
  0-439-89965-6

*Point*

POINTCKL